Beyond the Tempest

Viti Lee Tackett

Book III
A Roseanna Series Novel

Song: *Drifter, Come Home* written and recorded by John Houston. Used by permission of John Houston Publishing. ASCAP

Acknowledgements

Thanks to Lois Hulse, my friend and former art instructor, for so graciously painting the picture for the front of the book. She took time to paint it, (on very short notice) even though she was right in the middle of teaching art classes.

Thanks to librarians, Anna Bates and Lavaun Smith, for all their help with the research I needed for this book. They went beyond the call of duty to obtain this information, sending all the way to Texas for part of it.

Thanks to Jason Martin, a young minister friend, for allowing me to use his special technique of preaching and also one of his sermons as a pattern for one of the characters in the book.

A special thank you to my family and friends for your love and support, and, especially for your prayers. You make my life better just by being here.

Dedication

I dedicate this book to my husband, Floyd, and our children, Randy Tackett, Terry and Melody Tackett, Cindy and Donnie Hines. We have walked through many "valleys" together, and, together, we have weathered many storms. Even though our 'ship' has been tattered a few times, we have always managed to go beyond the tempest to the safety of the harbor. Thank you all for being there. I love you.

Beyond the Tempest
Skies are still blue,
Beyond the Tempest
The harbor's in view,
Beyond the Tempest
Hope springs anew,
Beyond the Tempest
Dreams do come true.

Chapter 1

"Mommy, you promised." Isabelle's lips trembled as tears stung her eyes.

"I know, baby, but I may have to break that promise," Roseanna said gently, pulling her daughter into her arms. "I don't know about you and Daddy both being gone for five whole days."

"Did I hear my name?" Brad asked, walking in just then.

"Daddy," Isabelle cried, running into his arms. "Please tell Mommy it's okay if I go with you."

Brad picked her up in one arm and put his other arm around his wife. "Second thoughts, sweetheart? I'll take good care of her, I promise."

"I know you will, honey; it's just the thought of both of you being gone."

"You could come with us," he offered.

Roseanna laughed. "I can just picture that," she said. "If I go, Mama and the girls will want to go; Belle doesn't relish being separated from Jesse, so she would come along and bring the kids, and of course, Grandma wouldn't want to be left behind..."

"The picture *is* getting a little crowded," Brad said laughing. "So, what's the answer sweetheart, do you want me to stay here?"

Love for him swelled in Roseanna's heart. He would give up his trip to keep from causing her pain. Dear, sweet

Brad. That was part of his great strength; the way he could put his feelings aside and think of others.

Brad, Daddy, and Jesse had been planning this fishing trip off the southeastern coast of Florida for weeks. It was spring break so Daddy was taking Lee along. Isabelle put in to go too. She argued her case vehemently. Lee was six years old and she was *almost* six years old; if he was big enough to go, she was big enough to go.

Roseanna was the only one who objected to the idea. She pointed out that Isabelle was a little girl and a fishing trip with the guys was no place for her. This reasoning sounded feeble, even to Roseanna, and she finally agreed to let her go. But now, when it was almost time for them to leave...

Roseanna looked at the two of them standing there. She saw the pleading look on her daughter's face and a hint of disappointment in Brad's eyes. This trip meant so much to them. She couldn't take that away.

She leaned over and kissed Brad. "My darling husband, I love you for thinking of me, but I don't want you to stay here. You go and have a wonderful time. Isabelle can go, too."

A smile covered Brad's face.

Isabelle jumped down out of his arms and hugged Roseanna. "Thank you, Mommy," she squealed happily. "I'm gonna go pack my stuff."

"Honey, you're already packed," Roseanna reminded her.

"Maybe I forgot something," she exclaimed, skipping off to her room.

"She sure is excited about this trip," Brad remarked as Isabelle disappeared from view.

"She's excited about going with you," Roseanna told him. "She's such a daddy's girl."

Brad smiled again. "I'm so blessed having two wonderful girls in my life." He pulled Roseanna close and kissed her.

"We're the blessed ones, Isabelle and me, having a great guy like you taking care of us." Roseanna snuggled closer to him. "Bradley Lefourche, I love you so much, I can't imagine my life without you in it."

"I love you, too, sweetheart, with everything inside me, and I truly believe God created us especially for each other. He gave us a special love that will last for all of eternity."

The prospect of spending five days without him overwhelmed Roseanna. "Oh, Brad," she cried, "I'm missing you, already."

"I don't have to go, honey," he said. "I can stay here with you."

"No, baby, you've looked forward to this trip and you need a break. I want you to go; but Brad, please don't ever leave me again. I can't survive without you."

"I can't survive without you, either, Roseanna, and I promise that from now on we'll never be separated from one another."

He kissed her and they stood there in each other's arms, spellbound by the greatness of their love; a love that neither time nor distance could ever erase.

Finally Roseanna spoke, breaking the spell. "It's getting late, I've got to fix supper, and you need to double check your list and make sure everything is ready for the trip tomorrow."

"You're right," he said, kissing her again. "But I don't want to let you go. I want to hold you like this forever." He sighed. "My arms will miss holding you."

"My arms will be empty without you, too," she said, "and they will be right here waiting when you get home."

The sun was barely peeping up through the horizon the next morning when Jesse's van pulled into the driveway of the parsonage.

"They're here! They're here!" Isabelle shouted, jumping up and down with glee. She ran to the door and let them in. "Grandpa, I'm all ready to go!" she exclaimed, running into his arms.

"I can see that," Ellis LeBlanc said, giving her a big hug and kiss.

Isabelle ran over to Jesse and tugged at his sleeve. "Let's go, Uncle Jesse. I'm ready."

Jesse looked at Roseanna and noted the tears misting her eyes. "I think Mommy needs a little more time to say goodbye," he whispered, leaning over to give Isabelle a hug.

Isabelle, with her loving ways and sunny disposition was a favorite with everyone. She had Roseanna's long brown hair and million-dollar smile; Brad's deep blue eyes, that sparkled like pools of clear blue water; and a bubbly personality, that delighted all those who knew her.

Ellis LeBlanc looked at his daughter and saw the tears too. "Honey, are you all right?"

"Oh, Daddy, I can't bear the thought of being away from Brad and my baby. Even though it's just for a week, it seems like an eternity."

Brad walked in from the bedroom with the last of the luggage. "I guess this is it," he said, taking Roseanna in his arms. "I'm going to miss you, sweetheart." He kissed her and she burst into tears.

"I'm sorry," she sobbed. "I wanted to be brave, but I'm just a big baby." She clung to Brad, kissing him over and over. "Have a wonderful time, honey, and don't mind my tears."

"I left Belle crying, too," Jesse remarked, with a tone of sadness in his voice. "It was hard to go off and leave her like that."

4

Brad nodded. It was hard leaving his precious Roseanna behind. Was the trip worth it? "Sweetheart, I could stay here," he said, almost hoping she'd say yes.

"Brad, honey, I'll miss you and Isabelle, but I want you to go. Now, get out of here before I change my mind." She pulled Isabelle into her arms and kissed her again and again. "You be a good girl and mind Daddy, and Grandpa, and Uncle Jesse."

"Mommy, I'll miss you," Isabelle said, tears welling up in her eyes; her lips trembling as she fought to hold back the tears. "I love you, Mommy," she cried as she climbed into the van and sat down beside Lee.

Daddy kissed Roseanna. "Thank you, for this beautiful boat you bought for us. This is going to be the best fishing trip ever."

"I want to thank you for the boat, too, Roseanna. It's such a generous gift," Jesse said, kissing her on the cheek as he climbed into the driver's seat.

Brad lingered, holding her in his arms. "Oh, baby, it's tearing my heart out to leave you. Maybe, I shouldn't go. I can't imagine enjoying this trip when I'll be missing you so much."

"Bradley Lefourche, you'd better enjoy this trip or you'll have to answer to me when you get back. Don't you go worrying about me either; I'll be fine. I have plenty of things to keep me busy, and I'll get to spend time with Belle, Mama and the girls, and Grandma. We're going to have lots of fun so you'd better have a good time, too." She kissed him, hoping he wouldn't sense her reluctance to let him go. "I love you, now, and for always," she whispered in his ear.

"Throughout all eternity," he whispered back, kissing her and climbing into the van. "I love you." He mouthed those words, throwing her a kiss as the van pulled out onto the dirt road, and headed away from Roseanna.

Roseanna felt a catch in her heart as she watched them drive away. She waved until all she could see was the big shiny boat hooked on behind the van. She didn't know anything about boats, so the men had picked it out. "A real beaut" was how they described it. She watched until they disappeared from sight and then walked back into the house. A lump, the size of a baseball came up in her throat, tears ran freely down her face. She could let go of her emotions now, and she did, falling across the bed and crying 'til there were no tears left inside her. She felt like a wrung-out dishrag as she lay there wondering how she could survive the next five days without the two people she loved most in the world. "This will never do," she mused, dragging herself to her feet. "I've got to stay busy."

This would be the perfect time to do her spring cleaning so she got out buckets and mops, dust cloths and polish, and everything else she needed, and she tackled the job head-on. It was getting dark outside when she finished the tasks she had set out to do. As she put the cleaning supplies away, she realized she had not eaten all day. She was too tired to cook, so she raided the refrigerator for leftovers. She found cold chicken and fruit salad. "This will have to do," she mumbled, getting a roll from the breadbox and pouring a big glass of tea. She didn't think anything had ever tasted so good.

She took a shower and put on her pajamas. As she got into bed, she suddenly remembered. She was the speaker at the Sunday morning service tomorrow. How could she have forgotten? She had not even studied. She dragged herself out of bed and opened her Bible. She read a few scriptures, but nothing inspired her. Why had she agreed to do this? When Deacon LaPree came down with a bug, yesterday, that confined him to bed, Brad had asked her to speak. "There's nothing to it," he had said, "easy as pie." He'd better be right.

Roseanna tried to concentrate but her brain was too tired to think. Her eyes were heavy and her body was aching all over. She sighed. The first mistake she'd made was to let Brad talk her into doing this; the second mistake was not studying before she did all that housework. Now she was just too tired. She'd have to get something in the morning before church. She closed the Bible, got into bed, turned out the light and was asleep almost as soon as her head hit the pillow.

Chapter 2

Roseanna stood before the congregation, the next morning, nervous and unprepared. She had overslept and only had time for a quick glance through the Bible as she hurriedly downed a cup of coffee. Her gaze fell on a familiar scripture. She would use that.

Now, standing here, wondering what to do, Daddy's words from the past, came to her: "write what you feel; sing from your heart." That had worked for her songs; maybe it would work now.

"Brad asked me to speak this morning and he told me it was 'easy as pie'. Well, maybe for him---but I'm standing here shaking in my shoes."

"Bless her, Lord," resounded through the sanctuary, as the congregation prayed for this young woman whom they all loved deeply.

"All of you know that I am not a preacher so this will not compare to what you're used to hearing, but this morning I'm going to talk to you from my heart. I've chosen a very familiar passage, and one of my favorites. Please turn to the 23rd Psalm." As she read the verses with meaning, she felt a calm come over her.

1. The Lord is my shepherd; I shall not want.
2. He maketh me to lie down in green pastures: He leadeth me beside the still water.
3. He restoreth my soul: He leadeth me in the paths of righteousness for his name's sake.
4. Yea, though I walk through the valley of the shadow of death, I will fear no evil: for thou *art* with me; thy rod and thy staff they comfort me.

5. Thou preparest a table before me in the presence of mine enemies: thou anointest my head with oil; my cup runneth over.
6. Surely goodness and mercy shall follow me all the days of my life: and I will dwell in the house of the Lord forever.

"The Lord is my shepherd, I shall not want," Roseanna stated. "That pretty well sums up my life. All the good things the Psalmist mentions here; the green pastures, the still waters, the table set before me; God has given me these things and much more. Do I appreciate His goodness, do I thank Him enough for all those good things, or do I take them for granted? Do I take God for granted? He has abundantly blessed me with a wonderful husband and daughter, a good family, and friends like you. He has given me only good things in my life, and I bask happily each day in those blessings. It's easy to be happy when everything is going my way; but what about when the storms come and I feel the tempest around me, how would I react then? I don't know." She read from Psalms again.

"Yea, though I walk through the valley of the shadow of death, I will fear no evil." She hesitated a moment. "I'm not there, yet. I'm not sure I ever will be. Walking in the shadows frightens me; thoughts of being tossed about in the tempest scare me to death." She hesitated again as tears welled up in her eyes. "Brad is there. He's already been through quite a few valleys and has come out victorious. When the tempest rages around him, he can get beyond the tempest, to the safety of the harbor, with faith and confidence. I asked him, once, how he did it; if it was because he knew that God was waiting beyond the tempest. 'Sweetheart,' he answered, 'God is not waiting for us beyond the tempest: God is in the tempest with us. That's how I make it through'." Tears were rolling unbridled down Roseanna's face now as thoughts of

Brad raced through her head. "Brad has so much faith in God that he can battle any force that comes into our lives, and I've become accustomed to leaning on his faith to see us through. Brad is my strength. I can get through any valley or storm as long as he is there with me." She paused momentarily. "I realize now, that I must find that faith for myself; I can no longer depend, wholly, on Brad's faith to see me through. I'm praying today for strength to be able to handle the bad times if they should come my way, to be able to walk through the valley of the shadow...without fear, just God and me. I know I've got to learn to trust in God for myself. The Lord is *my* shepherd---I can lean on Him for strength because He is there for *me.*"

Roseanna closed her Bible. "My cup truly runneth over today. My heart is filled with overflowing love for my Lord and Shepherd, " she said. "Let's stand and sing praises to Him." She picked up her guitar and began to sing. The sweet spirit of worship filled the hearts of the people as shouts of praise went forth to their King.

"Brad will be very proud of you," Belle remarked as they walked over to the parsonage after the service ended. "He couldn't have left the church in better hands."

Roseanna nodded. "You're right, but it wasn't my hands, it was God's hands."

"Give yourself some credit, Sis, you had to study and prepare," Belle said.

Roseanna laughed. "Actually, I didn't. I spent all day yesterday cleaning house. By the time I finished and remembered the sermon, I was too tired to study. This morning I overslept and only had time to glance briefly through the Bible. I found the 23rd Psalm and God did the rest."

"However it came about it was a great service," Belle said.

"Yes, it really blessed me," Roseanna commented, then added, "We'd better hurry and get changed and get over to Grandma's. We don't want to face her wrath if her dinner gets cold."

Belle giggled. "You're right. Mikey, come here and put on your play clothes," she called. "We're going to Grandma's house."

Mikey came running as fast as his four year old legs would carry him. He loved going to Grandma's house.

"He's so much like his daddy," Belle remarked, looking proudly at him.

"Yeah, with those big brown eyes and that warm smile, he's gonna break a lot of hearts one day," Roseanna said, giving her nephew a big hug. She picked Annie up and carried her into the bedroom to change her. "I think Annie looks like you, except for the blonde hair, of course," she yelled to Belle.

"We haven't figured out where she got that mop of blonde curls," Belle yelled back, laughing. "Reckon the hospital gave us the wrong baby?"

"No, aside from the blonde hair, she's a LeBlanc all the way," Roseanna answered, as she finished dressing her namesake in a yellow playsuit. "Rose Anne, you are simply gorgeous," she said, planting a kiss on the baby's forehead.

"Rise and shine," Brad said, as he shook the Pooh Bear sleeping bag gently. "Time to get up."

"Is it morning already? Isabelle asked, peeping out from inside the sleeping bag. "I'm not through sleeping, yet."

"That's 'cause you're a *girl*," Lee said, "and girls are sissies."

"Are not!" Isabelle exclaimed indignantly.

"Are too," Lee affirmed more stubbornly.

"Are not…"

11

"Okay, kids, stop your bickering," Brad said, in a gentle voice, putting his arms around them. "We're here to have fun."

Lee stuck his tongue out at her and Isabelle glared at him with a 'drop-dead' look in her eyes. Brad shook his head. These two had been bickering ever since they left home yesterday. He didn't have a clue on how to get them to stop fighting.

Setting up camp was not going so smoothly either. Thanks to a flat tire and Isabelle and Lee wanting to stop so often, they had arrived at the campsite late last night and everyone had grabbed their sleeping bags and gone straight to bed. Now, they were up, early, rushing to finish the job so they could get out on the boat. They began with putting the tents up. Each man had different ideas on how it should be done, and they were getting nowhere fast.

"We'll each put up our own tent," Ellis suggested. "That way, we can do it the way we want to."

Brad and Jesse nodded. That was a good idea. But they soon found it was not so easy putting up a tent all by yourself. By the time the tents were up and the supplies all in place, it was almost eleven o'clock.

"Roseanna will be starting her 'sermon' just about now," Brad mused aloud. He had promised to pray for her; and he had intended to really intercede on her behalf, but he only had time for a quick 'Lord, bless her', before jumping in the van with the others and racing off to find a restaurant. Too many hours had passed since supper last night; they were all starving, and their nerves were on edge. Isabelle was whining and Lee was getting more hateful with each passing minute.

Frazzled nerves, empty stomachs, and bad moods, kept them snapping at each other on the way to the restaurant.

12

"We'll all feel better after a good meal," Jesse commented, feeling the need to get everyone back on good terms with each other; after all he was a counselor, and that was his job.

They finally found a restaurant and decided on what to eat. The men chose the 'big man's breakfast' with sausage, bacon, eggs, pancakes, butter and syrup, and a order of biscuits and gravy on the side, along with a huge pot of coffee. The kids wanted hamburgers and fries, with sodas to drink.

"Isabelle, you can have the burger and fries, but only if you have milk to drink," Brad told his daughter firmly.

"The same goes for you, Lee," Ellis LeBlanc stated.

The kids made faces at the prospect of milk instead of sodas. "How about milkshakes? Lee asked, hopefully.

Both fathers agreed and the orders were placed. After what seemed like an eternity the food was set before them.

True to Jesse's prediction, they did feel better after eating. The men apologized to each other, and their spirits were high as they boarded the boat for the long awaited fishing trip. After making sure Isabelle and Lee's life jackets were secured firmly around them, they lifted the anchor and set sail.

The men sat lazily on the deck, fishing, eating donuts, and drinking the mugs of coffee they had brought along. The kids had individual boxes of juice to drink. The warm afternoon sunshine bathed them in all its brilliance.

"Life don't get much better than this," Ellis commented, and Brad and Jesse agreed.

The afternoon wore on. The white puffy clouds off on the horizon had turned to ugly black clouds and they were swiftly moving out over the water. The sun went behind the clouds and the wind off the water brought a chill to the air.

"Kids, put your coats on," Brad yelled, as the three men reached for theirs.

"My coat don't fit over this," Lee said, taking off his life jacket.

"You're supposed to keep that on," Isabelle scolded.

"I don't have to," he taunted, "but you do, 'cause you're a girl."

"Don't either," she said defiantly, taking off her life jacket and laying it on top of his.

"We'd better head back to camp," Ellis said worriedly, as he surveyed the dark clouds moving ever closer and the waves dashing against the boat. They hurriedly pulled their fishing rods out of the water and started securing everything.

The storm hit with a fury. The winds howled, the rain came down in torrents; the waves dashed angrily against the boat and tossed it about as if it were a piece of driftwood.

Isabelle was frightened. She stood, to run to her daddy, but just then a big wave hit the boat, tipping it to one side. "Daddy!" she yelled as she was swept over the side of the boat, and into the angry waters below.

"Isabelle!" Brad screamed in horror, jumping in after her.

Jesse yanked off his coat, and quickly untied his sneakers and kicked them off. Ellis LeBlanc started to jump in too, but Jesse stopped him.

"You take care of the boat, and Lee, and contact the Coast Guard," he yelled as he dived into the water. "I'll get Brad and Isabelle."

Jesse battled the fury of the water as his eyes searched for them. Not seeing anything, he dove under the water and swam around, frantically looking for any sign of them. Nothing. He came to the surface, gasping for breath; and staying only long enough to catch his breath, he dove

14

again. This time he searched underneath the boat in case they had gotten caught on it's bottom. Again and again, he searched, coming up only when he had to, and staying above water only long enough to catch his breath. He had covered a radius of several yards from the spot where they went overboard when the turbulence of the waters swirling around him, total exhaustion, and a knowing inside him, forced him to give up his search. He climbed, wearily, back on the boat.

"They're gone," he muttered, gasping for breath. "They're both gone."

Chapter 3

"Grandma sure outdid herself with that dinner," Roseanna remarked as she and Belle walked back to the parsonage late that afternoon.

"Yeah, I love her Cajun fried chicken, and her special recipe for mashed potatoes," Belle said. "Do you think she'll ever share her secret recipes with us?"

Roseanna laughed. "Not as long as she's breathing. She might leave them to us in her will."

Belle laughed too. "She certainly doesn't want any competition when it comes to her cooking."

"Grandma cooks good," Mikey said, as he walked along beside them, holding on to Roseanna's hand.

"You're living proof of that." Roseanna smiled. "I counted three chicken legs that you ate and I could have missed a few, and how many pieces of chocolate pie did you put away?" she asked, playfully tickling his ribs.

He giggled and squirmed away from her. "This many," he said, holding up two fingers.

"Where do you put all that food?" she asked, shaking her head.

"I promise, I do feed him at home; I guess my cooking just doesn't compare with Grandma's," Belle said, stopping momentarily to check on Annie, who was sleeping peacefully in her carriage.

"Isabelle's the same way," Roseanna said. "When we go to Grandma's to eat, you'd think I never feed her at home."

As they walked into the churchyard, a chill went through Roseanna. She shivered. "Whew, it suddenly got cold out here," she said, shaking all over.

Puzzled, Belle looked at her. "It's not cold out here," she said. "You must be coming down with something."

Roseanna nodded. "Probably the same bug that Deacon LaPree has," she said, walking into the house. She went to the closet and pulled out a sweater. "Maybe this will help."

"Do you think you need to go to bed?" Belle asked worriedly.

"No, I'm not going to spoil the big night we've got planned," Roseanna said. "Don't worry, I'll be okay."

Later, after the kids had been fed and tucked into bed, the two sisters made ready to enjoy the plans they had for tonight. They popped a pizza into the oven and opened bottles of their favorite soda pop. Roseanna fixed a salad and in a few minutes they were pigging out.

"I remember the time Jesse and I pigged out on doughnuts and coffee," Belle remarked, as she stuffed more pizza in her mouth.

"What was the occasion?" Roseanna asked. "I know Jesse wouldn't pig out for no reason."

Belle hesitated. Why had she brought that up? She couldn't tell her sister the truth; that they were celebrating Belle's heart being set free of the love she had for Brad. That was a secret she must keep hidden forever. "We were celebrating something special, I'm sure---it was a long time ago," she said, shrugging it off. She hoped Roseanna wouldn't sense that she was hedging the question.

They finished supper, rinsed the dishes and stuck them in the dishwasher; then they went down their list of things to do.

"Let's do the makeovers, first," Belle said excitedly.

They took turns encasing each other's faces in mudpacks. They painted, they polished, trying every new shade of lipstick and nail polish they could find. They tried different hair-do's, each one more ridiculous than the one before it. They giggled and laughed, and for a while it was as if the years rolled back and they were home again in the room they shared for so long, just being sisters; doing things that sisters do together.

"It's been too long since we've done things like this," Roseanna remarked, a touch of remorse in her voice.

"Much too long," Belle agreed. "Let's make a pact right now, that we'll get together, just the two of us, every month or so and have a 'Roseanna and Belle' night out."

"Sounds good," Roseanna said, "but right now I'm ready for some ice cream. How about you?"

"Bring it on," Belle answered. "So what if we have to give up food for a month, we're living it up tonight."

"I'll make my super-duper, ooie-gooie, all time special sundaes," Roseanna said. She got the ice cream dishes down from the cabinet and dipped three scoops of ice cream into each one. She poured on chocolate, caramel, and strawberry toppings and squeezed a big dollop of whipped cream on top. She sprinkled chopped nuts over all of it, topped it off with a maraschino cherry, and handed one to Belle. "My masterpiece," she added, bowing low.

"Thank you," Belle said, frivolously, taking a big bite. "Hmm, this is delicious. My compliments to you, madam."

They giggled and took their treats into the living room. They pulled out the family album they had borrowed from Mama and slowly turned its pages. Some of the pictures made them laugh; some made them cringe.

They came to the pages that held the school pictures. "Look at my first grade pictures," Roseanna lamented. "All my front teeth are missing."

"At least it looks better than this one," Belle cried. "The way my front teeth are sticking out over my bottom lip, I look like a chipmunk that just ate a persimmon."

"You sure were unhappy about something," Roseanna said, grinning, amused by Belle's description. "Do you remember what it was?"

"I haven't got a clue," Belle answered. "Wonder why Mama keeps all these awful pictures?"

"I don't know, but I think it's time a few of them bites the dust," Roseanna replied. "Do you want the honor or shall I?"

"Let's both do it," Belle said, taking the 'chipmunk' picture and tearing it into little pieces.

Roseanna followed suit and soon not one 'offensive' picture was left. "If Mama asks, we'll play dumb," she said.

"Oh, look, here's pictures of your wedding," Belle exclaimed, as they flipped through more pages of the album.

"See, how handsome Brad is," Roseanna said, running her fingers over the picture of him standing beside her at the altar. "He's so gorgeous in that tuxedo."

"You're no slouch yourself," Belle said, "I've never seen a bride as beautiful as you."

"I'll show you one," Roseanna said, turning some more pages. "Take a look at yourself in your wedding gown, Belle. You're absolutely breathtaking."

"It was a beautiful wedding, wasn't it? And we've got Jesse to thank for that. I wanted to get married in Paris and spend our honeymoon there, but Jesse talked me into waiting and having a big wedding here. I'm so glad he did, 'cause otherwise there would be no beautiful pictures to commemorate our special day." Belle sighed. "Talking about wonderful guys, Jesse is right up there at the top."

"Right along with Brad," Roseanna agreed. "Let's face it, Sis, we've got the two most wonderful guys in the universe."

"You always knew you loved Brad, but, I didn't always know my heart, and I almost substituted physical attraction for true love. Remember, I only realized it was Jesse that I loved a few minutes before I was to become Mrs. Lance Pecot. I really hated myself for hurting Lance that way. But as things turned out he wasn't ready to get married either, and we've remained good friends through it all."

"Do you think Lance will ever settle down and get married?"

"I don't know," Belle answered. "I think he enjoys being the most eligible bachelor in Paris."

"Lance would," Roseanna said, smiling as she thought of their dear friend. "I hope he finds what he's looking for."

"I hope so, too," Belle said. "I'll always have a special love for him."

Tears filled Roseanna's eyes as painful memories from the past went through her mind. "If things had turned out differently, I probably would have been married to the prince now, instead of Brad, and it scares me to death to think I could have gone through life without my precious Brad by my side. I thank God every day for giving him back to me. I love him so much. He and Isabelle are my reasons for living. I wouldn't want to live in this world, not even for one day, without the two of them." Tears were rolling down her face now. "Let's change the subject before I flood the living room with my tears."

"How about calling it a night?" Belle said, yawning. "It's getting late and my kids will wake up early in the morning, full of energy and ready for the new day.

"That's all right with me," Roseanna said, stifling a yawn. "I do feel a little drained."

Belle nodded. "Do you still feel sick, Roseanna," she asked later, as they got ready for bed.

"I still feel a chill, and my stomach is a little queasy; but I don't think I'm really sick. There's this strange sadness all over me and I feel empty inside. I guess missing Brad and Isabelle is settling down on me."

"Yeah, I miss Jesse too," Belle said. "It's like part of me is gone. Of course, I do have my kids with me and that makes it a little more bearable."

They prayed, then, crawled into bed. Belle was asleep almost immediately. Roseanna was sleepy but she couldn't go to sleep.

Another chill went though her as she lay there in the darkness. She pulled the covers up around her. She wished she could shake this feeling. She needed Brad here to hold her. Her arms ached to hold him. In three days they would be home, but right now, to Roseanna, those three days seemed like forever. She turned her back to Belle and wept, tears drenching her pillow. Weariness finally consumed her and she slept.

Chapter 4

Roseanna was sleeping soundly when a loud knock at the door woke her. Was it morning already? No, it was still dark outside. Who could be knocking on her door this time of night? Something must be wrong! Was it Earl's mother, had she taken a turn for the worse? Was it Grandma? Roseanna's heart stopped beating as she pulled her robe on and headed for the door. Belle was right behind her.

She opened the door and stood there, startled. "Daddy. Jesse. What are you doing here? Is Brad getting Isabelle out of the van?" she asked, then not giving them a chance to answer, she ran outside.

Belle could tell by their faces that something was wrong. She looked questioningly at Jesse. He shook his head. She ran into his arms.

"What's wrong Jesse? Please tell me they're okay."

Jesse pulled her close to him and held on to her with all his might. He shook his head again, tears streaming down his face. "They're gone, Belle. They're gone."

"Oh, God, no! she gasped, as her heart broke inside of her. She felt herself go limp in Jesse's arms.

"Brad, honey, do you need help getting Isabelle in the house?" Roseanna asked, reaching the van. She climbed inside. The van was empty, except for Lee sleeping in the back seat. "Brad? Isabelle?" she called softly. She jumped from the van and ran back into the house. "Where are Brad and Isabelle? Why did you come back without them? What's going on?"

Ellis LeBlanc took his daughter in his arms. "My darling Roseanna," he mumbled, his voice breaking.

"Daddy, if this is a joke, it's gone far enough. I want to know where they are, and I want to know right now," Roseanna demanded angrily.

Her father looked at Jesse with a plea for help in his eyes. This was tearing his heart out; he couldn't tell her; he just couldn't.

Jesse helped Belle to the couch and put his arms around Roseanna. He looked for words to say, but there were no words that would make it easier.

His voice faltered as he tried to tell her. "I'm sorry, Roseanna---there was an accident on the boat---a storm---Isabelle fell overboard---Brad jumped in to save her---I'm so sorry..."

"Are they hurt badly? Where are they? I want to go to them..."

Jesse shook his head. "Sweetheart, they're gone. We tried our best, but we couldn't save them."

"No," she screamed, beating him with her fist. "Why are you doing this to me, Jesse? How can you be so cruel? Why are trying to hurt me?"

"Roseanna, I would never hurt you, you know that."

"No!" she screamed again. "I would have known. I would have felt their pain." She fell limp to the floor. "Oh, God, this afternoon. It happened this afternoon. Oh, God, I did feel it," she whimpered as she remembered the chill that had gone through her and the sad, empty feeling that had enveloped her. "No," she said, shaking her head, determinedly, "I only felt that way because they were in danger. The coast guard has found them. They're safe now; I know it. Brad promised he would never leave me again, and he'd never break a promise he made to me. Call the Coast Guard, Daddy they'll tell you," she cried, walking over and shaking his arm. "You left too soon, that's all."

"Baby, we've been in touch with the Coast Guard all the way home. They searched and searched, but they didn't find them."

"Then, they'll have to search some more. Call them, Daddy. Tell them to keep searching. They can't leave them out there. They've got to find them. Call them, daddy, please. They can't leave Brad and my baby out there all alone."

Ellis LeBlanc dialed the number. His voice was strained as he talked to the man from the Coast Guard. "This is Ellis LeBlanc. Have you found anything?" He looked at Roseanna and shook his head. She snatched the phone from his hand.

"Please find my husband. Please find my little girl," she pleaded tearfully. "Their names are Brad and Isabelle. Please don't leave them out there; please bring them back to me."

The man's eyes filled with tears as he heard her words. He wanted to assure her that everything would be okay, but he couldn't. His voice broke when he answered her. "We're going to do everything within our power to find them," he promised, knowing full well that would never happen. He knew that between the strong currents, and the sharks, their bodies would never be found; but she didn't need to hear that.

"Thank you," she said feebly and handed the phone back to her father. He said a few words, then, hung up.

Roseanna felt herself suffocating. Her throat was burning; she struggled for breath. She had to get out of here. She bolted out the door without saying a word.

Belle started after her. Jesse stopped her. "Let me go," he said. "You're in no shape to go after her."

"I've got to go," Belle told him. "My sister needs me. You stay here with the kids. I'll be okay." She didn't wait for a response from him; she raced out the door after

Roseanna. She knew where she'd find her. She ran toward the bayou and stopped a few feet before she got to Roseanna's special place. She didn't want to disturb her; she only wanted to be there when her sister needed her. She stayed in the shadows and waited.

Roseanna fell to the ground by the big log underneath the oak tree; the same log she'd sat on with Brad the first day she met him. She knew even then that her heart belonged to him and always would. "Brad," she whispered, "I won't let them stop looking for you, my darling; I know you're out there, and I know Isabelle is with you; you'd never let anything happen to our little girl. Oh, baby, I can't stand the thought of you and Isabelle being lost out there alone, but don't lose hope, we will find you. Our love can overcome any obstacle; you said so. My love is reaching out to you and Isabelle, so hold on, my precious ones. Our love will bring you home to me." She wept bitterly as she thought of the fear and agony they must be going through; and she couldn't be there to help them.

Belle heard her weeping and ran to her. She fell down beside her and gathered her in her arms. "Roseanna," she cried. "I'm so sorry. I wish I could take your pain away, but I can't. Please, let me help you through this."

Roseanna drew her sister to her and they clung to each other. "Oh, Belle, why?" she cried. "Why did God do this to Brad and Isabelle, and to me?"

Belle couldn't answer that question, so she held her sister closer and wept with her. She remembered Roseanna's words at church this morning. She was praying for faith of her own, to be able to walk through the valley of the shadow---*of death*—"Oh, no, God, please don't take her there," Belle pleaded silently. "She's not strong enough yet. Please, let them find Brad and Isabelle---alive." Belle tried so hard to believe the thing she had just prayed for, but in her heart she knew… "Oh, God, what's going to happen to Roseanna? How's my sister going to get through this?" Belle stopped to listen when she heard Roseanna praying.

"God, I know You are the Father of this universe, and no matter where Brad and Isabelle are, they are not hidden from You. You can see them right now. Take them in Your arms and shield them from harm. Pick them up out of those raging waters and keep them safe; and bring them back home to me." She stood to her feet. "Let's go, Belle, maybe they've heard something by now."

Belle felt uneasy about Roseanna's prayer. She had sounded so sure that God was going to save them. What would happen when she had to face the fact that Brad and Isabelle were not coming back; that for some reason, God did not choose to rescue them. Could she survive that? Belle didn't think so. Would it be kinder to make Roseanna face the truth now, instead of allowing her to hold on to this false hope? She would ask Jesse; he'd know what to do.

When they reached the parsonage, Mama was there. She took Roseanna in her arms and caressed her. "Oh, my baby," she cried. "I wish I could take your pain on me, but I can't. I can only hold you in my arms and tell you how very much I love you, and that I will always be here for you, my precious girl."

"Mama, hold me," Roseanna whispered, as tears flowed down her face. Mama's arms had been a haven to her many times when she was a girl and needed a place to run to. She needed a place now; a place where she could escape the realities of what was going on around her. She stood there, in the comfort of Mama's arms, until she composed herself. Then she turned to Daddy. "Have they found them, yet?"

Daddy shook his head. "Sorry, honey."

"Let's all join hands and pray that God will protect them and bring them home safe to us."

Belle looked at Jesse. Mama looked at Daddy. Roseanna had not accepted the fact that they were gone. What would happen when she had to face the truth? While she prayed for the safety of Brad and Isabelle, they all prayed for her.

Mama went home soon after the prayer to tell Grandma and the girls before they heard it on the news. Ellis and Jesse had persuaded the Coast Guard to keep the accident a secret until they could get home and tell Roseanna, but now it would be all over the radio and TV. It would be hard enough on them, hearing the news from Mama; none of them could stand hearing it from a stranger.

The news of the accident spread swiftly through the bayou countryside. Brother Trosclair and his wife were the first ones to arrive at the parsonage. They held Roseanna and cried along with her. Soon all the folks for miles around showed up to grieve, along with Roseanna. It was hard to face the fact that their beloved pastor would never again preach in the little white church, and that Isabelle's happy laughter would never again be heard. Brad was more than a pastor to these folks; he was a part of every family under his care. It would take a long time for their broken hearts to heal enough so that they could accept another pastor. Through the course of the day, several voiced their feelings to Brother Trosclair. He promised he would fill the pulpit until they could get beyond their grief and accept someone else, no matter how long it took.

Miss Sarah and Miss Kathleen showed up by mid-afternoon. They had heard the news on TV and rushed to Roseanna's side. The trip from Alabama seemed unusually long and tedious today. The tears that stung their eyes, spoke of the pain that filled their hearts.

Roseanna's extraordinary calmness and peace amazed everyone.

"She's in shock," some whispered.

27

"It hasn't sunk in yet," others surmised.

But Roseanna was calm because she refused to believe that they were gone. Her heart wouldn't give them up, if they were dead, she would know it. They were alive somewhere out there and she would find them. That assurance was all that kept her going.

Later, after most of the folks had gone home, Brother Trosclair spoke privately to her. "Roseanna, we'll plan a memorial service for them, just let me know what you want..."

"Brother Trosclair," she said with a hint of anger, "how could you even suggest such a thing? They're coming back, so please don't mention a memorial service again."

"Roseanna, I'm sorry, I didn't mean to upset you." His brow furrowed with concern. "Call me if you need me, sweetheart," he said, kissing her on the forehead.

The next few days Roseanna was constantly in touch with the workers she had hired to continue the search after the Coast Guard gave up. Rescue helicopters scanned the area for miles around the spot where they had gone into the water, hoping to catch a glimpse of them, and divers searched beneath the waters.

It had been seven days since the accident and still no sign of them. Roseanna put in a call to the workers, telling them to keep on searching indefinitely; to spare no expense, to use all the latest technology; whatever it took, for as long as it took. She would not give up looking for them; but she had to face facts. If they had not been found by now...all the people who loved them needed closure.

Tears were streaming down her face as she dialed Brother Trosclair. "Plan the memorial," she said, and hung up the phone.

Chapter 5

Roseanna sat in the little white church between Brad's Mom and Dad. They had lost their only child, and the only grandchild they would ever have. The unbearable pain they felt showed in the lines of their faces. Her heart ached for these two precious people, whom she had come to love as if they were her own parents. She had to find the strength to put her grief aside long enough to help them.

William Bradley Lefourche Sr., a man of great strength and character, sat, his head bowed, his shoulders stooped; the pain in his eyes mirrored his great loss, his only son---gone. He ran his hand through his salt and pepper hair. Suddenly, he felt so old. He wept, realizing that he could never again reach out and touch his beloved Brad. He'd never have another chance to tell him how much he loved him, and how proud he was of him. Had he told his son these things the last time he saw him? He couldn't remember. Oh, if he could only go back...those words would have been spoken.

His mind went to his sweet little Isabelle. It was as if he could hear her precious words ringing in his ears. "Pa-Pa, I love you," she'd say, as she climbed upon his knee and kissed him. He wanted to remember every word she'd ever said to him, every time she'd ever smiled at him, all their special times together "Oh, God, don't let me forget one thing about my precious son and granddaughter," he prayed, as the tears ran down his cheeks.

Janet Lefource sat there, quietly weeping for the son she loved so much, the son she longed to see, and hold in her arms, and whisper words of love to him as she did when he was a baby. Her deep blue eyes, which usually sparkled from the joy she felt inside, were now clouded by the pain she felt in her heart and the tears she shed, as words from the past; Brad's words, raced through her mind.

"Mommy, here's some flowers. I picked them myself," he said, proudly, handing her the bouquet of wild flowers, and smiling happily.

"Mom, I hit a home run today and knocked in the winning runs," he exclaimed, excitedly, returning home from a state playoff, where they had won the championship.

"Mom, I leaving home. I'm confused about a lot of things and I need to figure them out for myself. I love you and Dad, and I will be back as soon as I get my head on straight," he said, right after his graduation from high school.

"Mom, God has called me to preach and I'm going into the ministry," he told her with a glow in his eyes that let her know he had gotten his head on straight, and could now begin a journey through life that would bring him happiness and contentment.

"Mom, I've met the girl I'm going to marry. Her name is Roseanna, and you're going to love her." She had never heard such passion in his voice.

"Mom, we're going to have a baby. You're going to be a grandma!"

"Isabelle," she whispered, as thoughts of her little granddaughter flooded her heart. "My precious baby," she sobbed, "Nana loves you…"

Roseanna heard her words and pulled her close and they wept together, over the loss of the two people they both loved more than life itself.

Brother Trosclair spoke with tender love as he talked about the fine young man who had captured the hearts of all the people entrusted in his care, and everyone else who knew him. He wiped tears from his eyes as he spoke of Isabelle, the little girl who had come into their lives for such a short time and spread sunshine into each life she touched. "To know Brad and Isabelle was to love them," he said, his voice faltering as tears ran unbridled down his face. "I know there are others here who want to pay tribute to them," he added, swallowing hard, over the lump in his throat.

Maurice was the first to go forward. "This is not easy," he began. "Brad was like a son to me. I knew, even before I met him, that he had to be someone special, for Roseanna to love him so much; and through the years I've found out for myself just how special he was. He really cared about people. He took the problems of other folks on his shoulders, just as if they were his problems. He sacrificed his comfort to comfort others, and he did all of this without complaining. My life is enriched from having known him and I feel honored today to have called him my friend. And little Isabelle, what a joy she was. I will cherish her memory and the happiness she brought to me. How blessed I was to have these two in my life. Brad, Isabelle, our hearts are saddened by your absence; we're going to miss you both. God-speed, my friends, as you walk with God into that wonderful place that is waiting for you. We'll see you again, someday, and up there, we will never have to say these sad good-byes again." He wiped the tears away as thoughts of Brad and Isabelle; and the family he'd lost all those many years ago flashed through his mind. He understood the intensity of Roseanna's loss and the pain that filled her heart, a pain that would never go away. He walked over and embraced her warmly. "I love you, child," he whispered, "and I'll be there for you if you ever need me."

Kent and Mavis went forward and spoke of their love for Brad and Isabelle, and for Roseanna. Minister colleagues spoke of Brad's work and the high esteem they had for him. Old acquaintances from back home in Mississippi relived the fond memories of the times they had spent with Brad. Folks from the bayou tearfully shared their feelings of love for Brad and Isabelle, and, of the great loss they felt.

Roseanna knew that words of praise and love were going forth in honor of Brad and Isabelle, but she really didn't hear them; she was here in body; but her thoughts, mind, spirit and heart; the parts of her that really mattered, were lost in the fog somewhere; and only an empty shell of the person that she used to be, was sitting here today. Suddenly she noticed that everyone was standing up, and she realized the service was over. She heard herself thanking everyone for coming, and for the kind words of love and respect. Then she turned to Brad's parents.

"Would you like to spend the night with me?" she asked, thinking of the long drive ahead of them.

"Thank you, honey, for asking," Janet Lefourche said, "but I think we need to go home; there's some things we have to come to grips with, and home is the only place we can do that."

Roseanna hugged her. "I understand," she said, kissing her fondly on the cheek. "Please call if you need me. I love you, Mom and Dad." She walked to the car with them.

Brad's father put his arms around her and drew her close. "You're all we have left now, Roseanna. You'll always be a part of our family. We love you and will always be there for you."

She embraced them and waved until they drove out of sight. She felt even more empty inside as she watched them drive away; it was like losing Brad all over again.

Kent, Mavis and Maurice had to catch a plane back to Nashville as soon as the service ended. Roseanna clung to them and wept. It was hard saying good-bye to these dear friends, who were an important part of her life. The others at the memorial service offered their condolences and left to go to their various homes.

"I wish I could stay longer, Roseanna," Angelina said, embracing her sister. "But I have some big-time exams this week and I must get back to school."

"Don't worry about me, honey, I'll be okay," Roseanna said, wiping away the tears that were running down Angelina's face.

Angelina had always dreamed of being a doctor, which seemed like an impossible dream for a girl from the bayou. When she graduated from high school, as a graduation gift, Roseanna had given her four years tuition at the college of her choice; with a promise to fund the extra years of study it would take for her to become a doctor. She also gave her money for all the extras she would need. That left Angelina free to concentrate on her studies instead of having to work to support herself.

"I don't want to leave you," Angelina cried as she thought of the pain Roseanna was going through. It wasn't fair for her to be suffering this way when she gave so much happiness to everyone else. Angelina clung to her sister. "I love you, Sis, and I can never repay you for all you've done for me."

"You just go and become the best doctor ever; that's all the payment I'll need."

Daddy drove Angelina to the airport. Mama and the girls went along to see her off.

Belle and Jesse stayed with Roseanna. Lee didn't want to go to the airport, so he stayed with them. Belle took Roseanna into the kitchen to try to get her to eat something.

Jesse noticed that Lee was unusually quiet; that something seemed to be bothering him. He lifted the young boy onto his lap. "What's wrong, Lee?" he asked.

"Nothin'," Lee mumbled and tried to climb down out of Jesse's lap.

"It helps to talk about it," Jesse said, holding on to him gently.

"Ain't nothin' wrong," Lee replied, his lip trembling. He wiped a tear away. "And I ain't cryin' either."

"There's nothing wrong with crying," Jesse assured him. "When you're sad, it's good to cry; it makes you feel better on the inside."

"I didn't mean to do it! I didn't mean to do it," Lee cried, burying his face in Jesse's shirt.

Jesse's brow wrinkled with concern. What was this child hiding that was tearing him up on the inside? "What did you do, Lee?"

"I killed her," he sobbed. "I killed Isabelle. I love her, but I killed her."

Jesse couldn't believe what he was hearing. "What makes you think you killed her?"

"My life jacket," he whimpered, "I took it off, so Isabelle took hers off too, and she got drowned, and it's my fault."

"Listen to me, Lee, I was out in those waters; it would have made no difference if she'd had her life jacket on, those waters were so strong, even a life jacket would not have saved her. It's not your fault she died."

Belle walked in. She was crying. "Honey, I need to talk to you."

Jesse gave Lee a big hug and set him down out of his lap. "What's wrong, Belle?"

"Roseanna is insisting that we go home. She's says she'll be okay here by herself, but I don't know. She won't eat anything, and she's not sleeping."

"I'll talk to her," he promised and headed off for the kitchen. Belle followed.

"Roseanna, about us leaving…"

34

"I insist on it, Jesse," she said, before he could finish his sentence. "You've been away from your practice much too long. Your patients need you."

"Our concern right now is you," he said. "We'll be here as long as you need us."

"That's just it, Jesse. I don't really need you to stay. I need to be by myself right now. I've got some things I have to deal with, and I've got to do it alone. Please go, I'll call you if I need you."

"Are you sure Sis?" Belle asked.

"I'm very sure. Don't worry about me, Belle, I'll be fine."

After they left, Roseanna stood, looking around the place that had been home to her for almost seven years. The home she'd shared with Brad; the home she loved. It had been a haven to her, but now it seemed strange, and so empty. The love and laughter that had filled these rooms had been hushed, and an unwelcome quietness had taken their place.

She was drawn into Isabelle's room. A cry came from her lips as she stood there, looking around at all of her daughter's things. The dolls lined up neatly on the canopy bed, with the pink covering and bedspread. Isabelle loved pink. She ran her hand lovingly over the bed and plumped up the pillows. Through eyes blinded by tears, she saw Pooh Bear lying on the floor beside the bed. He was Isabelle's favorite toy. She'd never left him on the floor if she hadn't been so excited about the fishing trip. Roseanna picked him up and laid him on the bed, amid the dolls and other stuffed animals. She went to the closet and pulled out a red dress, with a ruffled skirt and a big bow in the back; Isabelle's all time favorite dress; she would have worn it every Sunday but Roseanna wouldn't let her. Now, she wished she had let Isabelle wear it as often as she wanted to. She held it close to her and rubbed it across her face. Tears streamed down her face as she thought of her little girl who would never again wear the dress. "Oh, my precious baby, how am I going to live without you? I miss you so much. Oh, if I could only hold you in my arms again, I would never let go of you." Her heart felt like it was going to explode inside her. She ran stumbling from the room.

She ran into the bedroom that she had shared with Brad, and fell across the bed, sobbing hysterically. Waves of loneliness swept over her as she longed to be in Brad's arms and feel his tender kisses. "Oh, sweetheart, why did you leave me? You said you'd never leave me, you promised Brad. Oh, my darling, how can I go on without you? My heart cries out just to see you, my arms ache to hold you, oh Brad, I can't survive without you." She could almost see him standing there, smiling at her, the way he so often did, for no reason, except that he loved her; he'd see her across a crowded room, he would smile, and suddenly even a good day would become better. As she lay here where they had shared so many intimate moments, she could almost feel his arms around her. She picked up his pillow and held it close to her. She could smell his cologne on it. A feeling of nausea swept through her. She threw the pillow down and ran out of the house. She had to get away from here. She couldn't face these memories, not yet. She got in the car and started driving. She ended up at a lake several miles from the bayou. In some strange way she felt close to Brad and Isabelle here.

She waded out into the water. Suddenly all the anger shut up inside of her exploded with a fury.

"Why, God?" she screamed. "Why did You take them from me? Why did they have to die? You could have saved them, Lord, why didn't You? I trusted You, I begged You to watch over them, but You didn't. You let them die alone, out there in those raging waters. How could You do that to Brad and my baby? They must have been so scared.

I hate You, God! I hate You!" She waded deeper into the water. "Take me, too, I want to die!" The water was now up to her waist. "Come on, God, send those raging waters, and let me die here, the same way You let my family die. Please, God, let me die." Her voice was lowered and pleading now as she waded deeper into the water. It was up to her shoulders. "If You won't take my life God, then I will." She started to take a step forward, a step that would put the water over her head.

"Mommy!" It was as if Isabelle's voice vibrated across the lake.

"Sweetheart, I love you for all of eternity." Brad's words ringing in her ears jolted her to her senses.

Eternity. "If I do this, I'll never see either one of them again," she cried in horror, then turned and quickly made her way back to the shore. She jumped in her car and sped away. She pulled into her yard and ran inside. Memories of Brad and Isabelle filled every inch of the parsonage. "I can't stay here," she cried, afraid of what she might do in the midst of all those memories. "I'll go back to Nashville," she exclaimed. Maybe she would find the peace there she so desperately needed.

She quickly wrote a note to her family telling them where she was going, and asking them to pick up her car at the airport. She called the airport and chartered a private jet. She threw a few clothes into a suitcase, grabbed Brad's pillow, a picture of him and one of Isabelle. She took the red dress from Isabelle's closet, picked up Pooh Bear, bolted out the door, jumped in her car, and headed for the airport.

Chapter 6

Roseanna went straight from the airport in Nashville to the hotel. She had called from the plane and made reservations. She would call Harriet in a little while; she wanted to start singing again as soon as possible.

She walked into the bathroom and splashed water on her face. She gasped, startled by her reflection in the mirror. Days without rest had taken its toll; bloodshot eyes, encased in dark circles, with a hollow, empty look, stared back at her. "I've have to go heavy on the make-up, and maybe dark glasses," she mused aloud. "I need to try to eat something," she added, as an afterthought. "Something light." She scanned the menu and called room service.

She drank the orange juice first, then, poured a cup of coffee. She spread apple butter on the cinnamon raisin toast and began to eat slowly. She had finished one slice of toast, when her stomach started to churn. She ran into the bathroom and threw up. She washed her face and poured another cup of coffee. Maybe, she could keep that down. She drank, cup after cup, until the pot of coffee was gone.

She took a shower and went through the motions of getting dressed. She rummaged through her luggage. Had she packed anything at all that matched? "It really doesn't matter," she mumbled, pulling out a pair of light denim capris, and a plain white knit top.

She dialed the phone. "Hello, Harriet," she said. "This is Roseanna. I'm back in Nashville and I want to resume my career. Do you think you can get me some bookings?"

"When do you want to start?" Harriet asked a little hesitantly.

"As soon as possible. Will that be a problem?"

"No problem at all, hon, if you're really sure about this."

"I'm sure, Harriet," Roseanna said. "I also need a place to live. Can you help me find something?"

"Do you want an apartment or a house?"

"I want a house, a big one, out from the city, preferably no neighbors close by. I'll also need a car."

Harriet's brow furrowed with worry. Roseanna coming here so soon after the accident; her desire to be secluded---that didn't sound good, but Harriet didn't press the issue, instead she said, "I'll get right on it."

"Thanks, Harriet," Roseanna said, gratefully. "With you on the job, it's as good as done."

She called Mavis next and told her that she had moved back to Nashville and of her plans to resume her singing career. "I'll need a whole new wardrobe for tours and personal appearances," she said.

"What did you have in mind?" Mavis asked.

"Something suitable for country music, but not flashy; and no bright colors. How soon do you think you can have at least a couple of outfits ready?"

"With Sara helping, it shouldn't take long," Mavis said. "Of course, I'll need you to come in, so we can go over some styles for the rest of the wardrobe."

"Thanks, Mavis, I'll try to get in soon," Roseanna said, starting to hang up the phone.

"How about later today?" Mavis asked quickly. "Come out to the ranch and we'll go over some ideas for the wardrobe, then you can have dinner with us."

Roseanna hesitated. "I-I don't know. It's pretty short notice, for you, that is, to have to cook for company."

"Nonsense," Mavis said. "I won't take no for an answer. I'll invite Maurice, and he can pick you up on his way here."

Roseanna couldn't get out of it gracefully so she accepted the invitation, then sighed as she hung up the phone. She wasn't in the mood to be around people, not even dear friends, like Kent, Mavis, and Maurice. There would be too many reminders of happier times; times they had all shared together, when Brad and Isabelle were still--- alive. The words stuck in her throat. Her head was throbbing. She took a pain tablet and laid down on the bed to rest. She closed her eyes.

The angry waves dashed against the rowboat with all its fury. Roseanna rowed with all the strength inside her; her arms ached, her muscles cried out for relief, but she had to keep rowing; she had to find Brad and Isabelle, she had to save them.

"Mommy! Help me, Mommy!" Isabelle's voice was pleading, frightened.

"Sweetheart," Brad called, reaching his hands out to her, "we're here."

She could see them in the water close to the boat. "Brad! Isabelle!" she called frantically. "Hold on, I'm coming." She had almost reached them when the waves, surging violently, and foaming like a rabid dog, caught them up and swept them away from her.

"No!" she screamed, rowing hard against the turbulence, as she watched them being carried farther and farther away. A whirlpool caught her small boat, twirling it round and round, with a fury she could not overcome. "No! No!" she screamed in horror as Brad and Isabelle was sucked, helplessly, into the raging waters below and disappeared from her sight.

"No! No!" Roseanna screamed, waking up and opening her eyes. Her forehead was beaded with sweat; her hands were clammy and shaking. She ran to the bathroom and threw-up.

Someone tapped on her door. "Maurice," she whispered, running to let him in. She fell into his arms, weeping.

"What's wrong, child?" he asked holding her close.

"They were in the water, they were calling to me. I almost reached them, but they were swept away by the raging waters. I couldn't save them, Maurice, I couldn't save them," she screamed, her eyes flashing wildly.

He shook her gently. "Roseanna, it was a terrible nightmare, but you're awake now..."

"Awake or asleep, the nightmare is always with me," she cried, trembling in his arms. "They're gone, Maurice, they died in those horrible waters."

He held her close. "Roseanna," he said, "you can't handle this alone. Give it to God, child, let Him help you."

"I don't want any more of God's help. He's done quite enough for me already," she stated bluntly.

"You don't mean that," Maurice said, a tear rolling down his face. "God loves you, Roseanna, you know that."

"If this is a sample of His love, then I don't want any more of it. Now, let's get going. Mavis is waiting for us."

The conservation had ended. Maurice knew that there was no need to talk to her now. It was too soon for her to listen. The pain was too fresh. The hurt was too deep.

It had over a year since Roseanna had been to the ranch. Kent and Mavis had bought it when their son was about a year old. They had hired a couple to live at the mansion to be house parents to the girls that came there. Maurice stayed on as supervisor, and Samantha as his assistant. Sara lived there too, and helped Mavis with the dress shop. Sara had learned the dress design business and was on her way to becoming a topnotch designer herself. Stacy was still the counselor at the home. With everyone doing their jobs well, the home was running as smoothly now as when Mavis and Kent were there.

As they drove down the winding lane that led to the big white house, Roseanna apologized. "I'm sorry I yelled at you, Maurice. I know you were only trying to help."

He reached over and squeezed her hand. "It's okay, Roseanna. I understand."

Mavis ran out to meet them. She clung to Roseanna. "It's so good to have you here," she whispered.

The rest of the afternoon was spent looking at patterns and fabrics. "Make these up in subdued colors, I don't want anything bright or flashy," Roseanna said, handing several patterns to Mavis.

They joined Maurice in the den. Mavis brought in tall glasses of iced tea. They talked a while, then, Mavis looked at her watch. "It's almost time for Kent to get home," she said. "Excuse me, I'm going to finish dinner."

"Can I help?" Roseanna offered.

"No," Mavis answered. "Everything's ready. I just need to put it on the table."

Maurice stood to his feet to go help her.

"You stay right where you are," Mavis said firmly. "This is one time you're going to be a guest only."

She went to the kitchen. Roseanna sat, leafing through a magazine. Maurice sat quietly, a worried look on his face. An awkward silence filled the room. These two friends felt uncomfortable around each other, and could think of nothing to say.

Kent walked in. "Is that Maurice's car in the driveway," he asked, hurrying into the den. "Roseanna?"

"I'm here to stay," she said, before he could ask the question. "I'm going back to country music."

Kent put his arms around her. His heart broke for her. He wished he could protect her from the pain now, as he had protected her all those years ago, when he was

42

working undercover, to bring down J.T. Prince and the drug ring. He had learned to love her deeply; she'd become like a little sister to him, filling the gap that had been left in his heart when his own little sister was murdered by a drug dealer.

Roseanna had been in physical danger then, and all his years of training as a cop had made it possible for him to protect her; but this hurt that consumed her now... "Oh, God," he prayed silently. "Show me how to help her." He kissed her on the forehead. "Are you sure about this, honey?"

She nodded her head. "Right now, it's the only thing that makes any sense in my life. Don't worry about me, Kent. I'll be all right."

"Daddy!" Two kids yelled, bounding into the room and making a beeline for Kent. He scooped them up in his arms and hugged them lovingly. "How's my two favorite little people?"

"Daddy, I'm not little," Bo said, with disgust. "I'm six years old."

"I'm 'free,'" Beth said proudly, holding up three fingers.

Mavis came in and walked over to them. "Hey, hon," she said, giving Kent a kiss and announcing that dinner was ready.

As Roseanna watched them, a family so happy, so full of love for each other, her heart cried out for the family she lost. She only nibbled at her food. "Mavis, this meal is delicious," she said. "I wish I had a better appetite so I could do it justice."

"Just wait 'til we get to dessert," Mavis replied, smiling at Roseanna. "I made my special hot fudge sundae cake. It's guaranteed to bring back your appetite."

"My wife is a good cook," Kent bragged.

"And just think she learned it all from me," Maurice said, teasingly.

They laughed, then, everything got quiet.

During the rest of dinner, the conversation was strained and guarded. It was as if all of them were walking on eggshells, not saying much, for fear of saying something that would remind Roseanna of Brad and Isabelle.

Beth was sitting beside Roseanna. She tugged at her sleeve. "Is Isabelle weally in heaven?" she asked, with the innocence of a child.

Mavis looked in horror at Kent, then at Roseanna.

"Yes, she is in heaven," Roseanna said sweetly, "and so is Uncle Brad."

"I sorry she's gone," Beth said sadly. "I luv her."

Roseanna hugged Beth. "I know, honey, I love her too." She turned away so Beth wouldn't see the tears that were beginning to roll down her face.

There was a long pause. "Time for dessert," Mavis said awkwardly. She went to the kitchen to get it. Maurice followed to help her.

"How would you two like to eat your dessert in the den, and maybe watch your favorite video?" Kent asked.

"Yes," both kids exclaimed. They almost never got to eat in the den, and to watch a video too, was indeed a treat.

Kent got their bowls of hot fudge cake, put an extra big scoop of ice cream on top, and they went into the den. He put the video in, and walked back into the dining room. "I'm so sorry, Roseanna. She doesn't realize..."

"It's okay, Kent, really," she said. "I've got to get used to them being gone." Her words sounded brave, but she was dying on the inside.

The sadness in her voice tore at Kent's heartstrings. "Please, God, put some sunshine back into her life," he prayed silently.

44

Belle called Jesse at his office. "I'm worried, honey," she said. "I've been trying to call Roseanna all afternoon and she doesn't answer the phone. I'm afraid something is wrong."

"I'm with my last patient, now," he told her. "Be ready in about thirty minutes and we'll go check on her."

"Thank you, sweetheart," Belle said, and hung up the phone. She called the baby sitter, and set out the baby food for Annie's supper. She fixed a plate of Mikey's favorite foods, in case they didn't get back in time to eat.

Jesse exceeded the speed limit slightly on the trip to the bayou. He didn't want to worry Belle, but he was plenty worried. In the frame of mind Roseanna was in, anything could happen. "We shouldn't have left her alone," he fretted under his breath.

Her car was not in the driveway. They hurried up to the house and knocked on the door. When no one answered, Belle started to get the key from under the mat.

"Never mind," Jesse said, "the door's open."

"Roseanna never leaves without locking her door," Belle exclaimed in alarm. They walked in and found the note. "Oh, no," Belle cried. "She's gone, Jesse. What are we going to do? We shouldn't have left her alone."

Jesse pondered a moment. "Honey," he said thoughtfully, "Roseanna going back to Nashville might not be a bad thing. That's the only place she's ever lived without Brad and Isabelle. Everywhere she looks here, she's reminded of them. Maybe, there, it will be easier for her to come to grips with losing them."

"Oh, Jesse, I hope you're right," Belle sobbed. "When I think of my sister there all alone with her grief..."

"Belle, she's not alone," he reminded her. "She has Maurice, Kent and Mavis. They'll take good care of her."

"You're right Jesse. I'm going to call Mavis right now and see if she's heard from Roseanna. She dialed the number.

Kent answered the phone.

"Kent, this is Belle. Have you heard from Rosanna?"

"Yes, she and Maurice left a few minutes ago. They ate dinner with us."

"We just now found the note she left, telling us that she was going to Nashville. Is she okay?"

Kent sighed and hesitated a moment. "I don't think so," he said. "I'm really worried about her. I think it's too soon for her to make this decision to go back into country music. I don't think she's up to it."

Belle started crying and Jesse took the phone. "What can we do, Kent? Do we need to come out there?"

"Jesse, I don't think it would help. She's not ready to listen to anyone, not even Belle. We tried to talk her into living here with us, but she's determined to go it on her own. I think now, all we can do is to pray for her, and let her know we love her, and will always be here if she needs us. Try not to worry too much. We'll keep an eye on her and call you if we need to."

"Thanks Kent. I feel better knowing you guys are there." They talked a few minutes longer, then said goodbye. Belle started weeping uncontrollably. Jesse took her in his arms. "She will be all right, baby. We've got to believe that. God is going to watch over her..."

"Like He watched over Brad and Isabelle?" she cried.

A worried look crossed Jesse's face. Was Belle losing her faith in God? "Oh, Lord, help us all," he silently prayed, as he pulled her close and tried to comfort her.

Chapter 7

A month had passed since Roseanna came to Nashville. Harriet had got the ball rolling, and she had already appeared at the Grand Ole Opry and done a couple of concerts. It felt good to be back on the stage, singing again. To her fans, it was as if she'd never left. She had already bought a house and would be moving in as soon as the interior decorators finished with it. She had told them to do it in Victorian decor; and left the rest up to them.

She poured liquor from the decanter into a glass, and drank it down. She didn't really like the stuff, but it helped dull the memories, and that was what Roseanna needed now, as painful memories flooded through her. Today was her anniversary; today she and Brad would have been married seven years. Sobs racked her body as her mind went back to their wedding day and to the vows they had made. 'Til death do us part'...death...she hated that word...it was so final; so cruel. It had taken the very essence of her life away from her. "Oh, Brad," she cried, "I love you, baby, I need you. I can't face another day without you. Why did you leave me, sweetheart?" She poured another drink and fell across the bed sobbing until there were no more tears left inside her. The effect of the liquor consumed her and she fell into a fitful sleep.

She had not seen Kent and Mavis, or Maurice, since the night she'd eaten dinner with them. She loved them so much but she couldn't be around them, not yet. There were too many memories---too many reminders. They had invited her to visit again, but she had made excuses each time.

Belle and Jesse had called to see if she wanted them to come to Nashville, but she had asked them not to. Even the dearest people in the world to her couldn't help her now. She had to do this alone.

A month later, the call came from the interior decorators; her house was ready, she could move in right away.

Roseanna parked her car in the driveway and sat looking at the big colonial style house. A tear slid down her face, as memories took her back to the small parsonage she'd shared with Brad and Isabelle, the home where she had been so happy. Now, she felt cramped in small places, like she was suffocating. She walked inside. The house was decorated perfectly. If only she could appreciate it's beauty, but to her, it was just a place to live.

Harriet was not lining up tours, yet. "They take longer to plan," she explained, which was actually the truth, but she really had not tried, because she was worried about Roseanna, and whether she was able to go on extended tours. She had set up concerts and personal appearances in nearby cities, so that Roseanna never had to be away from home more than a few days at a time.

Roseanna had been in the house for a couple of weeks when the doorbell rang. She peeked out the window. It was Kent. She popped a breath mint in her mouth, she didn't want him to know she'd been drinking, then, she opened the door.

"Quite a place you've got here," he said, walking in and giving her a kiss on the cheek.

"Thank you, Kent," she said politely.

"Mavis sends her love, and we're wondering when you can get back over to see us. We miss you."

"My singing keeps me busy," she said.

"So busy that you don't have time for your friends," Kent remarked, bluntly. "We're all worried about you, Roseanna. Please let us help you."

This was not going to be easy, but it had to be done. "Kent, I love you and Mavis and the kids, but for now it's best if I stay away. Each time I see you, it brings back memories of Brad and Isabelle. It opens up the wounds, and, frankly, I'm not strong enough yet to deal with that. Please understand, and don't stop loving me. I need all of you, please don't give up on me." Tears misted her eyes.

He took her in his arms and held her close. "Honey, we could never stop loving you, and give up on you; not a chance. Just don't give up on yourself," he said, wiping a tear from her eye. "Roseanna, don't stay away from us too long. We've lost Brad and Isabelle, we don't want to lose you too."

She clung to him and wept. "Oh, Kent, I wish I was strong, but I'm not. I know my family at home needs me. They all loved Brad and Isabelle so much, and we need each other to help us through this awful time, but I just can't do it. I wish I could lean on you and Mavis and Maurice for the strength I need, but I can't do that either. I know you love me, and this is tearing you apart, but when I see you, all those memories come flooding back over me."

"Roseanna, we'll stay away, if that's what best for you, on one condition; if you ever need us, no matter what time of night or day, you will call and let us help you."

"I promise," she said, "and, Kent, thanks for caring."

He kissed her again and walked hurriedly to the car. "Oh, God, somehow, bring some sunshine into her life," he prayed earnestly. The longer she walked in the shadows, the harder it would be for her to come back to them.

When he left, Roseanna fell across the bed sobbing. She had wanted to reach out to him, today of all days, but she couldn't. Today was Isabelle's birthday. She would have been six years old. "It's not fair!" Roseanna screamed, picking up Pooh Bear and holding him close. They had given him to Isabelle on her birthday three years ago and he had become her favorite toy. "My baby," she whispered, as she fought to survive the heartrending pain that tore at her insides. "Oh, Isabelle, Mommy loves you so much and I can't go on without you, my precious girl."

All of her family had called today as they had on her anniversary, letting her know that they loved her and trying to comfort her in some small way. Did Kent remember? Was that why he came by? She wanted to be close to her friends again; she yearned to be back home with her family; but the pain in her heart kept her away from all those she loved.

She had a concert the next night in the city. She performed to perfection. When she was on stage, she was like a different person; she felt alive here, she could forget the past for a couple of hours while she was singing to her fans.

After the concert, the band was going out for drinks and invited her to go along. That would take a few hours off the long night that was waiting for her at home, so she went with them. There was lots of loud, noisy chatter, and even louder music. They ordered beer and hamburgers. Roseanna drank too much and was feeling a little wobbly.

"Come, let's dance," Billy said, pulling her to her feet. He was the new lead guitarist in the band and had only done a couple of concerts with them. He was very good looking; and he knew it. Roseanna tried to refuse, but he pulled her out on the dance floor. It was a slow song and he held her close while they danced. "I need some fresh air," he said, and led her outside. He pulled her close again, and kissed her forcibly.

50

She shoved him away. "How dare you!" she screamed, slapping him across the face and rubbing her hands across her lips. She started crying. "No one kisses me. I belong to Brad, and I always will." She ran into the club and found Jay. He had been the drummer in the band, when she was in Nashville before, and always played for her when she performed in the area.

He saw her trembling. "What's wrong, Roseanna?" he asked. "Did Billy try something?" There was anger in his voice.

She nodded her head. "Take me home please."

"Okay, just wait here a minute," he said, and walked over to Billy.

Roseanna couldn't hear what they were saying, but by the look on Jay's face, she didn't think Billy would ever bother her again.

When she got home, she went into the bathroom and washed her face with lots of soap and water. Her lips felt vile. She threw up. She picked up Brad's picture and held it close. "Oh, baby," she cried, "I let you down. I've violated all the principles you held dear. Brad, I'm no good without you. I need you here. Sweetheart, why did you leave me?" She cried herself to sleep, clutching the pictures of Brad and Isabelle in her arms.

"Mommy, help me. Mommy! Mommy!"

Roseanna sat straight up in the bed. "Isabelle," she whispered. "My baby." She poured liquor into the glass on the stand by her bed. She had to drown out these nightmares. The next several hours tottered between sleep, nightmares, and the bottle.

The ringing of the doorbell awakened her. "Go away," she mumbled, but it kept ringing. She pulled the covers up over her head to drown out the noise. It rang again and again. "Go away!" she shouted angrily, hoping

51

they heard. The doorbell stopped ringing. Roseanna breathed a sigh of relief.

Then she heard a loud pounding on the door. She jumped up and walked, fuming, toward the door. "What nerve!" she exclaimed, yanking it open.

The young man standing there smiled. He surveyed the young woman in the doorway; still dressed in the gown she had worn to the concert, her eyes bloodshot; her hair all mussed up and falling down in her face, a bottle clutched in her hand.

"Lord, why did You send me here?" he questioned under his breath. But aloud he said, "I'm Andy Winslow and I..."

"Whatever you're selling, I don't want any," she stormed. "You are a very rude person and I..."

"Oh, I'm not selling anything," he said sweetly. In spite of her outburst, he had to keep his cool. "I'm out canvassing the neighborhood, and I want to invite you to church."

"I don't go to church, not any more," she informed him and shut the door in his face. She started back into the bedroom when she heard another knock at the door. Angrily, she opened it again.

"I don't mean to bother you..."

"Then why are you?" she demanded furiously.

"The Lord told me to," he answered softly.

She knew he would not give up until he accomplished his mission so she motioned him inside.

"And just why would the Lord tell you to disturb me?" she asked, sarcastically.

He shook his head. "I'm still waiting on Him to tell me why. I just know He wants me to be here, I guess to invite you to church."

"Well, you've done what you came to do, so feel free to leave now," she said, rudely walking out of the room, feeling certain that she had seen the last of him.

Andy Winslow could not put the young woman out of his mind as he drove back into town. Why did she not go to church anymore; and why did God want him to visit her? He didn't accomplish one thing except to make her angry. The hopelessness he saw in those big brown eyes haunted him. What had happened in her life to put such sadness in her heart? He knew he had to try to help her. "Lord, show me what to do," he prayed, looking at the slip of paper in his hand. "Roseanna Lefourche, I'm going to find out all that I can about you before my next visit."

Chapter 8

The next day, Roseanna was quietly drinking a cup of coffee and planning songs for the concert that night. She had not written any new songs since coming to Nashville, so she had to get by on the old ones; her fans loved the old songs, so there had not been a problem, so far. She was strumming the guitar and singing softly, when the doorbell rang. At first she ignored it, but whoever was ringing it would not give up. "I'm coming," she yelled crossly, and opened the door. "I should have known," she muttered, looking into the smiling face of Andy Winslow.

"Hope I'm not bothering you," he said politely, "but I want to apologize for my rudeness yesterday."

"And what about your rudeness today?" she snapped. "I'm very busy, I don't have time for idle chit-chat. Whatever you've got to say, get on with it, and let me get back to my work."

He was somewhat taken back by her attitude. He understood it now, and that made her stinging remarks a little easier to take. "I-I guess I just want to say I'm sorry, and I'm also sorry that we got off on the wrong foot---the Lord sent me here to help you and I've messed things up, big time..."

"So you and the Lord think I need help," she snapped again. "The only help I need from you is for you to go away and leave me alone. I've got a concert tonight and I'm trying to get ready, so if you'll please excuse me." She slammed the door in his face.

Andy had a talk with the Lord as he drove back to town. "Lord, I know she needs some sunshine in her life, and you say, that I'm the one to help her find it; but everything I do just makes her more hostile. How can I get through to her? I want to help her, but how can I, when all she ever does is slam the door in my face." He thought back to what he'd found out about her. Poor kid, losing her family like that. He could see how that would make her bitter, and he could even understand why she would take her anger out on him; but her resentment towards God--- that scared him. "Father, show me the way to help her," he prayed. He'd start by attending her concert tonight.

Jay and his teenage son, Scott, gave Roseanna a ride to the concert. Jay didn't want her driving alone, on the deserted highway that led to her house, late at night, especially after what had happened with Billy. He didn't trust the guy. He'd keep an eye on him at the concert, but he'd feel better, knowing that she got home safely. Scott was in love with Roseanna, and to get to ride with her to the concert was like going to heaven without the dying part.

Andy sat, in the aisle seat, at the concert. Step one of his plan---he was here. Step two---escort her home from the concert---he didn't quite have that one figured out yet. "Lord, I need some help here," he muttered to himself. Then Roseanna walked out on stage. "Wow," he whispered. "Wow." He almost forgot his mission as he listened to her sing. The concert was half over when he suddenly remembered. He quickly wrote something on a slip of paper and motioned for an usher. "This is a request for Roseanna," he said, handing him the paper. Then he glanced upward. "I've done my part, Lord, the rest is up to you."

The usher handed the note to Roseanna as she headed back on stage after the dancers finished their act. "It's a request from a fan," he said, feeling honored that he had actually gotten to speak to her.

She ran out on stage. "Folks, I've got a request here from one of you, so I'll try to work it in right now," she said, reading the note. She blushed slightly, caught off guard by its contents. "Okay, where are you?" she said, trying to compose herself. "Stand up, wherever you are, Andy Winslow and take a bow. Folks, this is the most persistent young man that I've met in quite a while. I have been rude to him; I've insulted him; I've even slammed the door in his face a couple of times; but did he get the message--- obliviously not. He's back again. Shall I read the request?"

A loud round of applause and yells rent the air.

She read the note, amusingly. "Roseanna, may I please escort you home after the concert? Andy Winslow. Sorry, Andy, but I rode here with friends."

"That leaves you free to ride home with me," he blurted out. Why had he said those words? They certainly were not the words he would have used. *I sure hope you know what you're doing, Lord,* he thought.

Roseanna threw up her hands. "I give up," she said. "Meet me backstage after the concert and you can drive me home."

Yells of approval went forth from the crowd.

"Yes!" Andy said under his breath, giving the thumbs up sign to the Lord.

"I guess you know I couldn't gracefully refuse your invitation in front of all those people," Roseanna said, as they drove home after the concert. "I don't want you to get the wrong idea."

"Oh, I'm not getting the wrong idea," he assured her. "I'm sorry if I embarrassed you. Maybe, if we could just start over." He extended his hand. "I'm Andy Winslow and I'm very pleased to meet you, Roseanna Lefourche. I hope we can be friends."

"Friends? I don't think so," she blurted out quickly. Then she looked at him, really looked at him for the first time. He looked to be a couple of years younger than Brad. His dark blonde hair, a bit tousled, and falling slightly in his face, gave him a strong rugged look. His hazy blue eyes, that looked so innocently at her, and the big smile that usually covered his face made her feel she could trust him; and he didn't remind her of the past in any way, so maybe they could be friends after all. She did need a friend. "Well, we'll see," she said, recanting her earlier words, and shaking his hand.

Roseanna didn't relish the thought of being home alone so she invited him in.

"I'll make coffee," he offered, "just show me the way to the kitchen."

"You make a good cup of coffee," Roseanna remarked later, taking a sip from the mug he brought her.

"I have a lot of hidden talents," he said, grinning, then added seriously. "Roseanna, do you mind if I'm frank with you?"

"Do I have a choice?"

"When I was making the coffee, I noticed there was no food in the kitchen. If I may ask, what do you eat?"

"I haven't had much of an appetite lately," she replied. "I mostly drink those liquid meals in a can."

"They may be okay sometimes but you need more stable foods," he told her. "I know you've been through a lot, but..."

"How do you know so much about me?" she asked, sounding a bit upset.

"Yesterday, when I left here, I wanted to find out everything I could about you---don't get mad---but I sort of checked you out."

"I'm surprised you didn't already know, the way the news media pouches on my every move."

"I didn't know you were *that* Roseanna," he explained. "I did know about the accident and your family..." his voice trailed off as he saw the look of horror that crossed her face. "I'm so sorry, that was unforgivable of me to bring that up."

She started crying. "Why don't you ask that God of yours why He took them from me," she sobbed. "Maybe He'll let you in on the secret, 'cause He sure hasn't told me why."

Andy put his arms around her. "I don't know why bad things happen to good people, Roseanna," he said. "I wish I could take away all the pain you're feeling right now, but I can't, so please let me help you through it."

"How can you help me?" she asked. "Can you bring my husband back to me; can you put my little girl in my arms again?"

"No, I can't do either one of those things," he replied sadly. "I can only offer myself to you, as a friend, who will always be here if you need me."

"I'm sorry, Andy, I do need a friend, that is, if you're willing to put up with me."

"I'm willing," he said. "Now, let's have another cup of coffee, then I have to be going."

Andy left and Roseanna turned out the light and started for the bedroom, when a soft knock at the door stopped her. Thinking Andy had forgotten something, she opened the door. Billy was standing there, drunk, with an angry look on his face.

"We're going to finish what we started the other night," he groused, in a drunken stupor.

"You're drunk, Billy, get out of here or I'll call the police," she threatened.

He grabbed her. "I don't think so," he said, "and don't depend on lover boy to come to your rescue 'cause I saw him drive away. So it's just you and me, baby," he said, "and I'm in the mood for love." He kissed her roughly, again and again.

She screamed and tried to shove him away, but he was too strong for her. She begged him to leave her alone, but her pleas fell on deaf ears.

He forced her down on the couch and started tearing at her clothes. "No, please, no," she pleaded, but to no avail. She wept when she realized that he was going to have his way with her and there was nothing she could do about it.

Suddenly, a pair of strong hands yanked him off of her and slammed him against the wall; then those same hands started beating him to a pulp. They hit him over and over.

Roseanna jumped off the couch. "No, Andy, stop," she yelled, trying to pull him away from Billy. "He's not worth it. Let the police handle it now."

Andy gave him one final blow, that sent him sprawling across the floor, then, he picked up the phone and dialed 911.

Roseanna was shaking like a leaf. "He tried to rape me! He tried to rape me," she screamed in a voice filled with panic.

Andy took her in his arms. "I know," he said, "but you're safe, now."

Kent was working the night shift so he was on duty when the call came. "Roseanna," he whispered, racing to the squad car. With sirens screaming and lights flashing he sped to her house in record time. He jumped out of the car. "Go around back," he told the young officer with him. He cautiously walked up to the front door. "Police. Open the door," he called out. When Andy opened the door, Kent looked him over. Then he rushed to Roseanna's side and took her in his arms.

She clung to him, motioning to the man on the floor. "He tried to rape me, Kent. If it hadn't been for Andy, he would have."

"Get that scum out of here," he told the officer who had just walked in. "Are you okay, Roseanna?"

She nodded her head. "Thanks to Andy."

"I'm going to call Maurice to come stay with you, you don't need to be alone," Kent said, picking up the phone.

"Kent, don't bother him at this hour, I'll be okay, I promise."

"I'll stay with her," Andy offered.

Kent looked at the young man. "And just who are you?"

"Andy Winslow, a friend of Roseanna's."

Kent looked at Roseanna. "How long have you known this man?"

"I met him yesterday."

He looked at Andy sternly. "Don't think for one minute that I would trust Rosenanna's safety to a man she's only known for one day. Now I think it's time you leave."

"I beg your pardon, sir, but I'll leave when she tells me to leave," Andy said respectfully, but firmly.

Roseanna took hold of Kent's arm. "It's okay, really, I trust him. He's a man on a mission," she said. "The Lord sent him to take care of me."

Kent was even more determined than ever to get rid of this weirdo; he knew the kind; get close to young women, then use the Lord as a means of gaining their trust. "I'll walk you to your car, Andy," he said, opening the door. He escorted the young man to his car and waited until he drove away. He went back into the house. "I wish you'd let me call Maurice."

"Nonsense, I'll be fine, Roseanna replied. "I have a topnotch security system here. No one can get in unless I let them in. I opened the door for Billy thinking it was Andy."

"Well, you be more careful who you open the door to," he scolded gently. "And, about Andy, I'd watch out for him, too." He kissed her goodnight and left.

Dear, sweet Kent, always watching out for her. She wished he hadn't made Andy leave: now she faced another night alone. She sighed and turned out the light.

A soft knock sounded at the door. "Who is it," she called.

"It's Andy. Is the coast clear? Has he gone?"

She opened the door. "Oh, Andy, I'm glad you're here. How did you get back so quickly?"

"I didn't go all the way home," he explained. "I pulled off on a side road and waited 'til I saw car lights going in the direction of town; I was hoping it was the cop. Who is he anyway?"

"We go back a long way. Make another pot of coffee and I'll tell you the whole story," she said. "But first, let me ask you something, why did you come back before? Did you sense that I was in danger?"

"No," he said, "I came back to ask you something."

"What?"

"It's not important, now," he said. "Let's get the coffee made. I want to hear all about that policeman."

She told him all about Kent and how he worked undercover to bring down the drug ring that the prince was operating. She told him how she and Kent were both shot and how God spared their lives. She talked on and on about her life as a country music star and how she almost married J.T. Prince. She didn't mention her life with Brad; those memories were locked deep inside her heart; they were for her only, and too special to share. She yawned. "I'm so sleepy," she said. "Thanks for being here." She stood up to show him to the door.

"I'm not leaving you alone," he said. "What happened with Billy tonight is going to hit you hard later on, and I'm going to be here when it does."

"I'll be okay," she said. "You go on home. You've got to go to work tomorrow and the night is almost gone as it is."

"I don't have to get up early," he said. "I don't have a job to go to. Now, you go on to bed and I'll crash here on the couch."

She wanted to protest more, but she was too sleepy. She walked into the bedroom, changed into her nightclothes and fell across the bed. She lay there in the darkness, her thoughts running amuck. Who was this man in the next room? What did she really know about him? Were Kent's feelings about him right? Why did he want to know so much about Kent? Kent was a good judge of people; he had to be in his line of work. And, speaking of work, why did Andy not have a job? Where did he get the money to live on? Did he prey on women? He certainly had the looks and personality for it. He seemed so honest; but wasn't that the trademark of a con artist? He *had* kept Billy from raping her; did that prove he was an honorable man; or was he only protecting his territory? Why had she gotten so sleepy, after drinking all that coffee? Did he put something in it? What did he have in mind for her when she fell asleep? Fear seized Roseanna and she tried to force her eyes to stay open, but they were too heavy. "Brad, I need you, baby. Please, help me, Brad..." she mumbled as drowsiness enveloped her and she drifted off to sleep.

Andy was sitting in the recliner in the den. He was struggling with memories of his own; painful memories that tore him apart; voices in his head that tormented him. He clasped his hands over his ears trying to drown out those voices, but they would not be quieted.

Thoughts of the past, and of Roseanna whirled through his mind as he drifted off to a fitful sleep. What would she think if she knew the truth? What would she do if she knew that he had killed his wife?

Chapter 9

"Mommy, Mommy, Help me!" Isabelle's voice rang out through the mist that hovered over the water. Roseanna ran around the harbor, following the sound of the voice as it cried out time and time again. She could see Isabelle! She could reach her.

"Hold on, baby, I'm coming!" she shouted, reaching out her hand to grab hold of her precious little girl. She touched Isabelle's fingers, and was about to pull her up, out of the raging water, to safety, when rough hands grabbed her from behind and snatched her away from her baby. She turned to look into Billy's sneering face. "No!" she screamed, kicking and hitting him. "Let me go—my baby—I've got to save my baby!" But he stood there, laughing and holding her back. She watched in horror as Isabelle, not able to hold on, sank into the murky waters and disappeared from sight.

"No! No!" she screamed, sitting up in bed. She screamed over and over, as the scenes of the nightmare played through her head.

Andy awoke with a start when he heard the screams. "Emily," he whispered, jumping to his feet. He turned the light on and reality hit him. It wasn't Emily's voice he heard, he would never hear her voice again; she was dead. "Roseanna," he cried, rushing into the bedroom and gathering her in his arms. He shook her gently to wake her.

She saw him and started screaming again.

"It's okay, Roseanna, I'm here," he said in gentle tones. "It was a bad dream, but now it's over." He held her

64

and stroked her hair. "It's over," he repeated. He knew about bad dreams, he'd lived with them for years.

Roseanna didn't know if she could totally trust him, but she was glad that she was not alone. "Why do I keep having these awful nightmares," she cried out, clinging to him.

He shook his head. "I don't know. Maybe, it's because you can't face the horror of what happened to your husband and little girl when you're awake, and then all your fears come out while you're sleeping," he said thoughtfully, "or maybe, it's so you can learn to accept the fact that they're really gone, and begin the healing process; maybe you need to let go of them."

She pulled away from him. "I'll never let go of them!" she screamed. "In my heart they're still alive, and I will never give them up!"

"I'm sorry," he quickly said. "Please, forgive me for being so thoughtless." He knew how hard it was to let go of someone you loved; he also knew that Roseanna had to do it in her own way, in her own time.

"I didn't mean to take it out on you," she said. "I'm just so tired…"

"You lay down and go back to sleep. I'll sit here with you," he said, pulling a chair up to the bed and taking her hand in his. He held her hand until she finally fell asleep. "God, give her a peaceful night's sleep," he prayed, as he let go of her hand and walked back into the den.

When Roseanna awoke again, the smell of bacon filled the room. She pulled on her robe and walked into the kitchen.

"Good morning," Andy said, standing at the stove, spatula in one hand and a cup of coffee in the other. He poured her a cup. "Sit here," he said, pulling out a chair. "I was going to bring you breakfast in bed, but now that you're up, we'll eat together." He put bacon and eggs on their plates, took biscuits out of the oven, got butter and jelly from the refrigerator and sat down beside her.

"Where did all this food come from?" she asked.

"I went to the store while you were sleeping. I wanted to surprise you."

"Well, you certainly did that," she said. "I'm sorry you went to all this trouble, but I don't eat breakfast."

"This morning you do," he said. Then he bowed his head and said grace. They were just about to dig in when the doorbell rang.

"Who could that be so early," Roseanna pondered out loud.

"I'm already here, so we know it's not me," Andy said, grinning. "You sit still, I'll get it."

"You'd better let me get it. It's probably reporters. They must have heard about what happened last night with Billy," she said. "I can just see the headlines if they catch you here: 'Roseanna has handsome live-in lover.' I'll get rid of them." She opened the door. Maurice was standing there. She cringed. She'd rather have reporters find Andy here than to try to explain things to Maurice.

"You doing okay?" he asked, giving her a big hug.

She nodded. "Kent called you, right?" I told him not to worry you. I'm fine, Maurice, really."

"Come on, Roseanna, your breakfast is getting cold," Andy yelled from the kitchen, thinking she had sent the reporters away.

Maurice's eyebrow's raised in surprise and he walked into the kitchen. "Who do we have here?" he asked.

"I'm Andy Winslow," the young man said, standing up and holding out his hand. "I didn't think Roseanna needed to be alone last night so I stayed here, on the couch---in the den," he quickly added.

66

Maurice ignored the outstretched hand. "Kent told me about you, young man, and, that he had made it clear that you were to leave, so what are you doing here?"

"Maurice, sit down and have some breakfast," Roseanna said, taking his hand. "Andy went out and bought all this food and cooked this lovely breakfast, now let's don't let it go to waste." She would have to eat now, to buy some time before she had to face Maurice's questions.

"I've already eaten," he said, "but I will have a cup of coffee and these biscuits look good," he said, reaching for one.

Roseanna passed the butter and jelly to him, and then took a bite of her food. It was good. "Where did you learn to make biscuits like this?" she asked, looking at Andy. "Another one of your hidden talents?"

He grinned. "We chefs never divulge our secrets," he said, hoping she wouldn't spot the zip lock bag from the grocer's freezer that they had come in.

"We all love Roseanna a lot and look out for her well-being," Maurice stated, looking at Andy.

"That's good to know, sir," Andy replied.

"We wouldn't take it kindly if someone tried to hurt her in any way," Maurice continued.

"Neither would I," Andy said.

"Maurice, you don't have to worry about me, honest. I love you for watching out for me, but I can take care of myself; I'm not that naïve little girl that came to Nashville all those years ago; I've learned a few things since then." She walked over and laid her hands on Andy's shoulders. "Andy is my friend, Maurice. I trust him, won't you at least trust my judgment?"

"I trust you, child, but I know what you've been through and the toll it's taken on you," Maurice said, his voice shaky. "If you say he's okay, then I'll take your word for it, but we'll be keeping our eye on the situation; if we sense there's something wrong, heaven help you, young man."

Roseanna gave him a big hug. "Thank you, Maurice, it means a lot to me, knowing that you're on my side." She kissed him on the cheek.

"I've got to be going," Maurice said. "Remember honey, I'm only a phone call away if you ever need me."

Andy walked him to his car. The two men talked a while before Maurice left.

Roseanna hadn't told Maurice the qualms she had about Andy. If he had even suspected that she didn't trust Andy completely; that would have been the end of it. She'd check him out on her own, and if her suspicious were true; then she would tell Maurice. If not, she'd still have Andy for a friend.

Andy came back inside. "I think I convinced him that I'm not a total monster," he remarked. "Are all your friends so protective of you?"

Roseanna nodded and laughed. "If you think my friends are protective, just wait 'til you meet my family, especially Grandma."

"I think I would like to meet your family, even if they do give me the third degree," he said.

Roseanna blushed. Was he getting the wrong signals from her?

I need to be going too," he said, glancing at his watch, "that is, if you're sure you'll be all right."

"I'll be fine," she assured him, "but how do I get in touch with you, in case something comes up that I can't handle."

"Here's my card," he said, handing it to her as he walked out the door.

She waved to him as he drove away. Then she looked at the card. It had his name, address, and phone number. How strange, she mused, to have cards printed up if you don't have a business to advertise; unless, of course, he was in the business of selling himself to lonely women, who had nothing in life, except a lot of money. Did she fit in that category? She'd soon find out.

She tidied the house and stuck the dishes in the dishwasher. She smiled when she saw the zip lock bag that had contained the biscuits. She got dressed and headed into town. She was going to learn all she could about Andy Winslow; she'd start by finding out where he lived.

"Wow," she exclaimed, when she drove into the parking lot of the most exclusive apartment complex in Nashville. She checked the address to make sure it was right. "How can he afford to live here?" she muttered, but she knew the answer. Kent and Maurice were right about him. Tears misted her eyes as she wondered how many women he had taken advantage of. Did he use the same MO on all of them; pretending to be a man of God, or was that reserved only for her? He had found out that Brad was a preacher and used that to prey on her; knowing she was vulnerable. "How could he take advantage of my suffering?" she cried, feeling more alone now than ever, remembering what her life had been like before Andy came into it. The bottle had been her only refuge. She'd found a ray of hope in his friendship; she had even learned to laugh again. Now all of that was shattered. He was only using her. She spun out of the driveway and hurried home. She ran inside, locked the doors and pulled the blinds. She was safe here. No one like Andy would ever get to her again. She fell down on the couch, sobbing. Why did losing him hurt so much? She grabbed a bottle from the bar and poured herself a drink, then another, and another. "Well, old friend," she mumbled, holding the bottle close to her, "it's just you and me, now, baby." She poured glass after glass and drank it down, until in her drunken stupor, the pain left her. She finally passed out on the couch.

She was awakened by the telephone. "Hello" she mumbled, her words fuzzy.

"Is something wrong, Roseanna?" Andy's voice showed genuine concern.

"Everything is fine," she said, tartly, knowing that his so-called concern was fake.

"I'm leaving town for a few days; I don't know how long I'll be gone. My brother in Dallas has been in an accident and he's in intensive care; they don't know if he's going to make it..." His voice broke.

"I'm sorry, Andy, I hope your brother will be all right," she said, compassionately. "Don't worry about me, I'll be fine."

"I'll see you when I get back," he said and hung up.

"Oh, I can't believe I fell for his line again," she chided herself, realizing that it was just that, a line to get her sympathy, and to buy time to get out of town. "He knows Kent and Maurice is on to him. Boy, he's good, I'll give him that."

Pretending that his brother was sick, that was a stroke of genius; and to think she almost fell for it; she was still gullible, that's for sure. She thought she had learned her lesson with the prince; but no, she swallowed the line Andy threw her; hook, line and sinker.

Brad was the only 'real' man in her life, the only one she could trust one hundred per cent, and now he was gone. How could she get through the rest of her life without him? All the painful memories came flooding back as her heart cried out for Brad and Isabelle. She grabbed the bottle, walked into the bedroom, fell across the bed, and wept, seeking relief from the pain by pouring glass after glass of the liquor and drinking it down.

Chapter 10

Andy had been gone two weeks now. He had tried to call several times, but Roseanna let the answering machine take all her calls; then she returned the ones she wanted to; and she didn't want to talk to Andy.

The days had been long and painful without him. She had sunk even further into despair than before. She was no longer able to do concerts, and spent her days and nights totally alone. She'd been in Nashville five months and she was no closer to the peace she longed for, then when she first got here. Would there ever be peace for her. She didn't think so. There was no lighthouse beyond this tempest, shining it's light out to her; there was no hope left in her without Brad and Isabelle.

She took solace in the bottle as she had so many times before. She drank until the memories faded and, then, giving over to total exhaustion, she fell asleep.

"Mommy! Mommy, help me, Mommy!" Isabelle's *cries sounded out over the noise of the storm.*

"Sweetheart, we're here," Brad's voice, calling to her, sounded close by. She ran to the edge of the water. She could see them! She could get to them! She jumped in a small boat and rowed in their direction. "Hold on, I'm coming," she shouted into the wind; it echoed her voice over the waves. She heard them screaming again and looked. Sharks had them surrounded. "No!" she screamed, trying to fight off the sharks. She saw blood in the water and Brad and Isabelle disappeared from view.

71

"No! No!" she screamed, fighting with all her might. She opened her eyes. It was a nightmare, worse than the others, and so real. She couldn't get the picture out of her mind. She reached for the bottle of liquor. She threw it against the wall. "I can't take this anymore!" she screamed. "I've got to have peace; please, God, just give me some peace."

Brad's words echoed in her ears. "Sweetheart, God isn't waiting for us beyond the tempest, God is in the tempest with us..."

"So, where are You, God," she cried. "Why have You forsaken me? I need You." Tears were rolling down her face as the words of a new song started forming in her mind.

"When your road gets long and narrow—And shadows fall on every side,
When clouds roll in and rain starts falling—you search through the storm but there's no place to hide."

"That's where I am," she cried out. The storm's too strong. I can't get through it. I need a place to hide..." More words flooded through her mind.

"When the sea gets angry and frightening..."

"Brad, Isabelle," she whispered. No, I don't want to go there, don't take me there!" But the words kept coming.

"And lifeboats are useless in waters so strong..."

"No, please, no," she cried as more words came.

"And the wind in your sails takes you too close to danger..."

She clasped her hands over her ears to shut out the words, but they kept coming.

"Now, helpless and hopeless, you're alive, but alone."

"But they're not alive they're dead," she whispered, as another flood of tears streamed down her face. Then Roseanna knew: the song wasn't about Brad and Isabelle; it was about her. She was without hope; she couldn't make it

72

through those raging waters by herself. "I need help," she sobbed. Please, God, help me." More words came.

"There's a door always open, and a light always shining, a fire always burning in a place to call home; and there's Someone who loves you, who never will leave you; He's waiting here for you, so drifter come home."

"Lord, You were there in the tempest, with me, all the time, I just couldn't see You through my pain. I'm sorry, God; help me, please help me." She fell to her knees and cried out to the Lord.

Andy rang the doorbell, then, knocked on the door. Roseanna's car was in the driveway, the lights were on, so she must be home. Why was she not answering the door? He walked to the window and looked in; he saw her on the floor. He got the key from underneath the mat and opened the door. He ran over to her and took her in his arms. "What's wrong?" he asked, panic in his voice.

"Oh, God," she prayed as if she didn't hear the question; as if she didn't even know Andy was there. "I'm sorry I failed You, God. Please come back into my heart. I can't make it on my own. I need You."

Andy joined in the prayer as tears ran down his face. His prayers were being answered. God had sent him on a mission to help rescue Roseanna, and now it was happening. "Thank You, God," he whispered, his heart leaping with joy.

They prayed together until Roseanna's tears of remorse turned into tears of joy. "Thank You, Father," she said, then turned to Andy. "Thank you for praying with me," she said, "and for being here for me."

"This prayer helped me too," he said. "Roseanna, there are some things I've kept from you and I'd like to get them off my chest now, if that's okay."

"By all means," she said, knowing that now she could forgive him for betraying her friendship.

He led her to the couch. "I haven't been totally honest with you..."

"I know," she answered softly, "it's about how you make a living. I was upset at first, but now..."

"The way I make my living---I don't understand..."

"You know." She hesitated. It was hard to find the right way to say this. "The way you make friends with--- wealthy women-- and—they pay you for your—friendship."

"A gigolo? Is that what you think?" He was horrified that she would think such a thing.

"I saw where you live, it takes a lot of money to live there, and you don't have a job..."

He laughed. "Do you know who I am?

"You're Andy Winslow," she faltered, obviously missing something here.

"Winslow, as in Winslow Steel," he said. "My family is one of the wealthiest in the country and I have a very large trust fund."

Roseanna blushed a deep red. "I'm sorry, Andy, I misjudged you. I wouldn't blame you if you never wanted to see me again."

"Not a chance of that," he said, "but there is something I do have to tell you."

"Okay, I'm listening."

"There was this girl named Emily. I loved her like I've never loved anyone. We loved each other with the same kind of love you and Brad had, the kind that never goes away." A look of sadness passed over his face.

"What happened?" Roseanna detected the look, and sensed something had gone terribly wrong.

"We got married and had great plans for the future, kids and a big house; but for us, the future never came." A single tear rolled out the corner of his eye and down his face. "I killed her, Roseanna, I killed my Emily."

She put her arms around him. "You could never kill anyone. Tell me what happened."

"I was young and foolish. I wanted to live it up, with booze and fast, expensive cars. Emily liked the simple things. She never was impressed by all the money I had. She went to church every Sunday and tried to get me to go with her, but I didn't see the need of it. I wanted to live life to the fullest and tried to make her fit into my lifestyle. I bought this flashy new sports car, a real beauty, and I insisted that we go for a ride in it that Sunday and spend the whole day together, just the two of us. She usually wouldn't miss church but she was thrilled about us spending the day together. And what a day we had. We walked along the beach, holding hands. Emily had prepared a picnic lunch so we found a secluded spot, and spent the rest of the day eating fried chicken, potato salad, and the best chocolate cake ever; and talking about our future. We were going to start a family right away. We took the long way home so we could enjoy the scenery. Emily always found beauty in the simple things. We were on a deserted highway, or so I thought, and I decided to show her how fast the car would go. She asked me to slow down, but I was having too much fun, speeding along, checking out my new toy. I didn't see the car that had swerved into our lane until she screamed and then it was too late; my Emily died instantly. I walked away with only a few bruises. I never got to tell her I was sorry, or how much I loved her. I held her lifeless body in my arms until they came and took her away. I don't know why God took her and left me, maybe because she was ready to meet Him, and I wasn't. I wasn't charged in her death, but I was guilty; and perhaps I received the worst sentence of all; going through the rest of my life knowing that I killed her."

"Oh, Andy, I am so sorry," Roseanna cried, tears flowing down her cheeks. "But, you've got to know it was an accident, you didn't kill her."

"If I had not insisted that she come with me that day, if I hadn't been driving so fast, she would still be alive; and all the plans we made; that big house and the kids, could have been ours."

"Don't blame yourself, Andy. You gave her a wonderful day with the man she loved; you made her last day on earth a happy one. She wouldn't want you blaming yourself," Roseanna said, tenderly. "I blamed myself for losing Brad and Isabelle. If I had just asked Brad to stay home with me, he would have, and they would both be alive now..."

"You weren't steering the boat..."

"No, but I bought it for them. If they had not had such a fine new boat, they would never have gone on the fishing trip," she said, "so you see I have plenty to blame myself for."

The two friends held each other and wept; for the loves they had lost, for the guilt that each felt in those deaths, and for the empty place that would always be in their hearts; and they prayed for courage and strength to go on.

Andy wiped his tears, then Roseanna's. "You look peaked," he said. "Have you been eating or sleeping at all since I've been gone?"

She shook her head. "I haven't felt like eating and every time I slept, I had those terrible nightmares." She yawned and laid her head on his shoulder.

"I think your nightmares are over," he said, "but the matter of your health is another thing. I'm taking you to the doctor tomorrow."

He waited for her to protest, but she didn't say a word. He glanced down at her; she was sound asleep. He smiled. "You'll probably get the best night's sleep you've had in months," he muttered as he eased her around on the couch and put a pillow under her head. He kissed her on the forehead and sat down in the recliner, and he, too, was soon sound asleep.

Chapter 11

The next morning Andy told Roseanna again, of his plans to take her to the doctor. She protested slightly, but consented when he told her he already had made the appointment and she only had time to eat a bite and get dressed. She didn't have time to call anyone and tell them what had happened last night; that she was back on track with God.

"You can call them when we get back from the doctor," Andy said.

"Tell me, again, why you think I need to go to the doctor," she quizzed him as they were in his car heading for the clinic.

"You're run down, you haven't been eating, just barely sleeping; I think you need some medical advice on what steps to take to get your system back in shape."

The clinic was running pretty well on schedule that morning and she didn't have to wait long. "Come with me," she told Andy when they called her name.

The doctor checked her over, then ordered several tests, which took most of the morning. She and Andy were waiting in the doctor's office for him to talk with them.

"Roseanna," he said, "about those tests we run..."

"Is something wrong with me?" she blurted out. "Is it serious?"

"Well, there is something. I ran all those tests because I wanted to be absolutely sure before I say anything."

"What is it," she asked, her voice choking, afraid of what the answer might be. Andy reached over and took her hand.

The doctor hesitated. "This is usually good news," he said. "Roseanna, you're pregnant."

The color drained from her face. "No," she gasped, "I can't be---I haven't---" She turned to Andy in tears. "Could I have done this and been so drunk that I don't remember?"

He put his arms around her. He didn't know what to say. How would this affect her now that she was finally beginning to put her life back together?

"Relax, Roseanna," the doctor said. "You're six months pregnant."

"Six months---that means it's Brad's baby. I'm going to have Brad's baby," she said, tears streaming down her face. "But how could I be pregnant for six months and not know it?"

"You have been through a lot these past few months, and you haven't been taking care of yourself. You probably attributed the signs of pregnancy to the pain you felt in losing your husband and daughter."

"Doctor, what about my baby, will it be all right? Have I hurt my baby by not taking care of myself?" There was panic in her voice.

"We're going to check that out right now," he said kindly. " We're going to do an ultrasound. After this test we'll know a lot more about the condition of the baby, and also whether it's a boy or girl."

They hooked Roseanna up to the machines and ran the test. She watched on the monitor as the outline of the baby appeared. "Everything looks okay, as far as we can tell," the doctor her, "and you're going to have a little boy."

"A son," she said, dreamily. "Brad's son. Andy, I'm having Brad's son. He'd be so happy..." She started crying. "Why did he have to die? We wanted a son for so long. Now, he'll never know---why couldn't he be here to share this with me?"

Andy squeezed her hand. "Roseanna, I think Brad knows, and I believe he's thanking God this very moment for giving you that little boy, so you'll always have a part of him here with you."

The doctor spoke up "Roseanna, I think the baby is fine; of course, we'll have to wait until he is born to know for sure on some things. These next three months are critical. You're going to have to get on a good diet, get plenty of sleep and lots of rest. I want you to stay off your feet for a month, at least, and don't travel much until the baby is born, and no air travel at all. We want to give this little fellow every chance to come into this world, a happy, healthy baby. If you don't have someone to take care of you at home, I can get you into a nice facility where they will cater to your every whim."

A facility. That had a nasty ring to it. "I'll get someone to help me at home," she said, quickly. "I'll hire an army, if necessary."

The doctor laughed. "That won't be necessary. But I do insist that you find someone immediately. You're not to be on your feet much at all starting right now."

"I'll see that it's done," Andy promised, shaking hands with the doctor as they left his office.

"I'll hire a staff around the clock," Roseanna said as they walked to the car.

"Let me handle it," Andy said. "I don't want you worrying about anything."

"Thanks," she said. "That takes a load off my mind. Oh, by the way, the night you came back and rescued me from Billy; you said you came back to ask me something, but you never did. What did you want to ask me?"

"I wanted to ask you to come and sing at the center where I work."

"What kind of center?"

"It's a center where I do most of my ministry…"

"You're a preacher?" she asked in surprise.

"Yes," he said. "But I'm not what people normally think of when they think of a preacher. I don't preach regularly in a church. Most of my ministry in done in places like the center, and to kids who don't have very good odds of staying out of trouble; some are street kids, some are from poor families who can't give them much in worldly goods, some are from families who just don't care. The center is a place where they can come and play games and have fun with other kids, and where we can present Jesus to them in the only way they understand; through love and caring," he explained. "Well, anyway, after what happened that night, with Billy, I didn't think you'd be up to singing for a bunch of noisy kids."

"I'd like to go there and sing for the kids before I leave Nashville," she said.

"You leaving? The doctor said bed rest for a month," he reminded her.

"I'll stay here another month, but I'm going home to have my baby."

He fell quiet. "The doctor said no flying, so how are you going to get home?"

"I'll figure something out," she said. "Hey, I'm starving. How about stopping for a burger."

"It's good to hear you say you're hungry," he said, pulling into a drive- through. "We'll eat in the car, if that's all right," he said, determined to keep her off her feet.

"That's fine, as long as I get food, I don't care where I eat it," she said. "I'm eating for two now, and I've got a lot of time to make up for."

When they got home, Andy made several phone calls. "It's all set," he told her. "You'll have a live-in maid and a cook, who is also a nutritionist, so she will plan your menus, to make sure you eat well-balanced meals."

"No more burgers and fries?" she asked in a pouting voice.

"Probably not," he said, "but I'll try to sneak one in to you every now and then."

The maid, Nancy, and the cook, Louise, showed up a little while later. Nancy made sure that Roseanna was comfortable and then started cleaning the house. Louise went right to work in the kitchen, preparing the evening meal.

"It seems like they're really efficient," Andy said. He didn't know how true his words were 'til later that night when he came by to check on Roseanna.

"They're driving me crazy," she whispered, when he inquired how things were going. "When they realized who I am, they became like two different people, stumbling over each other to try to get to me first. I can't even go to the bathroom by myself. They have not let me take one step on my own. They've got to go."

Andy grinned. "Sounds just like what the doctor ordered," he said. "You've got to be careful, Roseanna."

"Careful, yes, but I'm no invalid." I want to do the things that I'm able to do and let them do the other stuff."

"Are you comfortable, Miss Roseanna," Nancy asked, walking in and fluffing the pillows, and pulling the cover up around her.

"Would you like a snack or something to drink?" Louise asked, right on the heels of Nancy.

Nancy, big-boned and tall, looked like she could tackle any job that came her way. Her short blonde hair, pulled back under the maid's cap that she wore, was perfectly styled. She had been given the awesome job of taking care of this young celebrity, who, in her opinion, hung the moon. She would do her job well; Roseanna would receive the VIP treatment, and much more.

Louise, short and pudgy, looked every bit the part of a cook, a good cook, who tasted each delicacy as she prepared it. Her grayish brown hair was pulled back in a bun and her chin set determinedly. If not for the warm glow in her hazel eyes, she would come across as stern and unfeeling. She'd been given a job to do; take care of Miss Roseanna, and no one was going to do it better than her.

"I'm fine," Roseanna told them, smiling warmly. They walked away obliviously disappointed. "See what I mean," she whispered to Andy.

"That's the price you pay for fame," he teased. "Adoring fans, worshipping at your feet."

"I could take a little less worship and a little more freedom," she said. "I'm not used to being pampered."

"You might as well get used to it, at least for the next month," he said, trying to suppress a grin. "To those two ladies you are royalty and will be treated as such."

"Can't you talk to them and get them to ease up a bit," she pleaded. "They won't listen to me."

"I'll give it a try," he said. "But, I don't think they will listen to me either. Let's face it, they adore you, and won't be deterred from doing their job by anyone."

"They've been here less than a day and I'm almost bonkers, what will I be a month from now?"

"Don't worry, sweetheart," he said, in his best 'Bogey' impersonation. "I'll come by, every now and then, and rescue you from the clutches of those females."

She laughed. "I'm gonna hold you to that," she said.

"How about right now," he said, "it's still early, we..."

"Time for bed, Miss Roseanna," Nancy announced, walking in just then.

"It's not even nine o'clock!" Roseanna cried in dismay. "I'm used to staying up later than this---much later."

"That was before you knew you were pregnant," Nancy replied. "We've got to take good care of that little baby, and you." She looked at Andy. "It's time for you to go, and let her get some rest."

He shrugged his shoulders and with a quick goodnight to Roseanna, headed for the door. He could see, now, what Roseanna meant. Those ladies had to go, or he had to find a way to outsmart them.

"I can do this myself," Roseanna protested as Louise and Nancy helped her into the bedroom. Her gown was lying across the bed, and the covers had been turned down. "I put clean linens on your bed," Nancy said proudly.

"And here's some hot herbal tea, it will help you sleep," Louise said, setting the cup of tea on the nightstand by the bed.

"Thank you both," Roseanna said sweetly. "I can take it from here. You can call it a night."

"Here's a bell," Nancy said, setting a big bell on the nightstand. "If you need anything during the night, just give it a ring and I'll come running."

"We both will," Louise added.

"Lord, help me to survive," Roseanna prayed when the two ladies left the room. She got dressed for bed and laid down but she didn't turn off the light. She didn't want to face the memories that would come in the darkness, memories of Brad and Isabelle. Even though God was with her now, those memories still hurt. When she fell asleep would the nightmares come back? She needed comfort. If

84

only she'd brought her Bible from home, but she had left in such a hurry. She'd ask Andy to bring her one. She wished he were here. "I'll call and talk to him," she muttered, dialing his number.

"Hello," he said.

"Hi," she answered. "I've got to talk to you or I'll go stir crazy. Can you imagine, me, laying here in bed at nine o'clock at night, with nothing to do but twiddle my thumbs? I don't know what I'm going to do for the next two or three hours, I certainly can't go to sleep this early. I don't even have a Bible to read."

"How about I bring you one?"

"Yeah, bring me one tomorrow when you come, and please come early, say, for breakfast."

"How about I bring you one right now? Do you think you can make it to the door and let me in."

"If the wardens don't catch me," she said, laughingly. "No kidding, I feel like a prisoner in my own home."

"Get dressed," he said, "I'm breaking you out of the joint."

Roseanna felt like a kid, sneaking out to meet her best beau. She got dressed quietly and turned out the light. She didn't want them thinking something was wrong if they woke up and saw her light on. She stopped breathing when she bumped into the nightstand and the bell tumbled off and hit the floor. It only made a muffled sound, on the carpet, but what if they were light sleepers. She jumped back into the bed and pulled the covers up over her. She lay there a few minutes and when she didn't hear a sound from either of them, she carefully got out of bed and tip-toed into the living room to wait for Andy. She saw the headlights of his car and gently opened the door without making a sound.

"I parked the car down the road so the noise wouldn't wake them," he whispered, picking her up in his arms. "I'll carry you to the car."

"You're as bad as they are," she chided. "I'd feel better walking to the car."

"I'm not thinking about you, I'm thinking about me," he said. "I don't want those ladies after me; it's bad enough I'm stealing you away in the middle of the night, if anything happens to you, they'd skin me alive."

"I see your point," she said, laughing. "Where are we going?"

"Since you're not supposed to be on your feet, I thought we'd go to my place," he answered. "I have plenty of popcorn and soda pop. I think I even have some juice for you to drink. How does that sound?"

"Sounds great," she said, as they reached the car.

He drove away slowly and as quietly as possible. Roseanna insisted on walking into his apartment and he didn't argue. It was only a few feet from where he parked the car.

"You have such good taste," she said, looking around the apartment.

"I can't take the credit for all of it," he said. "My mom picked out most of the furnishings."

"So much has happened since you got back from Dallas, I forgot to ask how your brother is doing."

"Thank God, he's going to be all right," Andy said. "He'll need a lot of physical therapy before he's completely well. The rest of the family stayed on in Dallas, but I felt like you needed me here."

"I'm glad you came back. I did need you. I wouldn't have gone to the doctor if you hadn't been here to insist, and my baby might not have survived."

"I'll fix the popcorn, and I've got some old movie videos, pick out one you like," he said. In a few minutes he came back with two bowls of hot buttered popcorn and a glass of juice for each of them. He sat down on the couch beside her and they settled down to watch videos of the "I Love Lucy" show.

"Is this okay?" she asked. "I'm in the mood to laugh."

"I love the Lucy shows," he said. "I catch all the reruns."

They sat, eating popcorn and laughing, 'til tears ran down their faces, watching episode after episode.

Suddenly Andy jumped to his feet. "I've got to get you home," he exclaimed. "It's after midnight!"

"Bring the rest of the videos when you come over tomorrow and we'll finish watching them," she said on the ride home.

"Okay, he said. "I have all the old Andy Griffith shows too. Do you want me to bring them?"

"Yes," she replied. "I love Andy and Barney and all the folks in Mayberry."

He parked closer to the house this time, but they were careful not to make a lot of noise, walking up to the door.

"Thanks, Andy, I had a great time…"

"Me, too," he muttered. Then he pulled her close and kissed her.

She pulled away, gently. "Andy, please don't ever do that again. My heart belongs to Brad; it always will, I will always belong to him. I could never love anyone in that way again." She was in tears. "I'm sorry, Andy, you mean a lot to me and I hope we can still be friends, but that's all we can ever be."

Roseanna, please forgive me," he said pain showing in his voice. "I've never kissed anyone since Emily. I don't know what came over me, and I promise it won't happen again, unless, and until we both want it to happen." He opened the door and stood there, making sure she was safe inside. "Goodnight," he whispered, as she waved to him. Then he shut the door and walked to his car. He had a lot of thinking to do before he went to sleep tonight.

Roseanna fought back the tears as she lay there in bed. Did she send the wrong vibes to Andy? Would he be back or had she driven him away forever? Was she being selfish wanting him in her life, but only as a friend? He deserved so much more than she was able to give. Should she send him away so he could find love with someone else? The thought that he might not be in her life anymore scared her. She didn't want to go back to that empty existence that was her life before she met him. But she could never give her heart to him; that would always belong to Brad. Maybe the kiss was just a reflex action and wasn't as big a deal as she was making out of it. She'd find out tomorrow.

Chapter 12

Andy came by early the next day with the videos. Roseanna could sense something different about him, like something weighing heavy on his mind. "We need to talk about last night," she whispered, not wanting Nancy and Louise to overhear. They didn't suspect a thing, and she wanted to keep it that way.

"Later," he said. "I've got some things to sort out; then we'll talk."

"I don't blame you for being upset," she told him. "Maybe I over reacted to the kiss. I don't want to lose you, Andy." She reached out and touched his hand.

"I don't want to lose you either," he replied. "Let me do some thinking and get back to you. I'll call you later."

She watched as he walked out and closed the door. Was the door to their relationship closed too? Had she shut it by her reaction to the kiss? Didn't she have to be honest with him? Didn't she have to tell him how she felt? Andy had become an important part of her life and she didn't want to lose him, but she couldn't pretend to have feelings that weren't there. She would always belong to Brad, completely; there would never be room for another man in her life. So where did that leave Andy? When would he call so they could talk? And, when they did talk, how would it play out? Would he walk out of her life for good? Her mind groped for an answer, but no answer came. She'd just have to wait and see.

In the meantime, Nancy and Louise kept the tug-of-war going, to see which one of them could do more for Roseanna.

"We've got to fatten you up," Louise said, and cooked meals fit for a king, keeping within the guidelines of nutritious foods.

Nancy catered to her every whim; royalty could not have been treated with more grandeur.

But for all their pampering and petting, Roseanna still felt lost and alone. The days, usually brightened by Andy, now stretched out long and empty. It was even worse when darkness fell. In the stillness of the night her heart cried out for Brad and Isabelle. She longed to see them; her arms ached to hold them. She reached out for them but only emptiness was there. Her heart broke when she thought of all the lonely years ahead without them. "Oh, God, why?" she cried, "Why did they have to die?"

A week later, the call from Andy came. "Roseanna, I'm coming over. It's time to talk," he said. He hung up without giving her a chance to say anything.

When he walked in the door, Roseanna tried to read his thoughts; but all she saw was a poker face; not a clue as to what he was thinking.

"I thought we'd go on a picnic," he said.

"Are you sure you're up to a picnic, Miss Roseanna?" Nancy's voice was filled with concern.

"I'll be fine," Roseanna said, "don't worry about me. The fresh air will be good for me."

"You'd better take a blanket; there's a nip in the air," Nancy said, not totally convinced that the picnic was a good idea. She went to the linen closet and pulled out a couple of blankets.

"I'll fix a lunch for you," Louise offered, and headed for the kitchen.

Andy stopped her. "I've got the food," he told her.

90

"Miss Roseanna is on a special diet," she informed him. "What foods do you have?"

"Fried chicken, baked beans, fruit salad and wheat rolls. There's bottled water and raspberry tea to drink," he said, keeping his fingers crossed that the menu would meet with her approval.

"Well, milk would be better; but I guess it will be okay," she said reluctantly, a little miffed that she didn't get to fix the picnic lunch for Roseanna.

"Those ladies sure are tough," Andy said, laughing, as they walked to the car. "They make me feel like I'm back in the principle's office, with him peering over those horn-rimmed glasses, trying to figure out what to do with me."

Roseanna laughed. "They can be intimidating," she said, "but I'm getting used to them now."

"Yeah, but they like you," he answered. "They only tolerate me for your sake. You should see the looks they give me."

Andy drove to a secluded spot on a nearby lake. He parked the car and spread a blanket on the ground for her to sit on. Then he brought the picnic supplies and put them on a red-checkered tablecloth that he had spread on the ground. "Let's eat first, then we'll talk," he suggested.

"Okay," she said, wanting to put off the bad news, if that's what it was, as long as possible. She thought the food would stick in her throat, but actually it tasted very good.

After they finished eating, he put away the picnic stuff, and sat down beside her. "Roseanna," he said, "I've spent the last week doing some soul searching and a lot of praying. I knew what I wanted to do, but I had to make sure it was the right thing for both of us; now I'm sure it's the right thing for me, and I hope it will be right for you, too."

Tears misted her eyes. "Is this goodbye?" Her voice choked on the words.

"Just the opposite," he said, taking her hand in his. "Roseanna, I want us to get married..."

A muffled cry came from her lips. "No, Andy..." He put his hand over her mouth. "Hear me out, please. I know your heart will always belong to Brad, and mine to Emily; but does that mean that we have to go through life alone, never reaching out for a different kind of happiness? I love you, Roseanna, and I think that you love me. I believe we could have a good life together. I'm happy when I'm with you, and I don't want to give that up."

"But why do we have to change anything?" she cried. "We're happy..."

"We're happy when we're together," he interrupted, "but what about the nights; all the memories that haunt us when we're alone in the darkness. Roseanna, I'm tired of facing those memories alone. I want you there with me."

"Andy, I could never consider marrying again," she said, weighing her words carefully, so not to hurt him. "In my heart Brad will always be my husband; he will always be alive to me. My head knows he's gone, but my heart will never accept it. I could never betray the vows I made to him. I could never give myself to another man."

"That's not what I'm talking about here," he explained. "I'm not expecting more from you than what you can give. I'm talking about two friends sharing a life together."

"Can't we be friends without marriage," she asked bluntly. "I don't see what one has to do with the other."

"Roseanna, we can't spend all of our time together without being married; even though we slept in separate rooms, what would it do to our reputations, to our witness for the Lord? What would people think?"

"I see what you're saying," she said, "and I do want you in my life. I love you and I need you by my side, but I can't take this step, Andy, I just can't."

"Honey, don't close the door on this," he said, taking her hand again. "Give yourself time to think about it, time to heal, time to decide what's best for the rest of your life."

"I'll be going home in a couple of weeks," she said, reflectively, "to the home that I shared with Brad and Isabelle. I've got to face the memories there. Only after I go there, and face those memories, can I give you an answer; but I think my answer will still be the same."

"I'm going to take you home to the bayou, Roseanna. I'm going to be there with you..."

"I have to do this myself, Andy, just God and me," she said, softly.

"At least let me drive you home, and stay close by until the baby is born," he said. "I don't want you going through that alone."

"Well, Grandma does have a spare bedroom, and I would feel better if you were there, so it's a deal."

"Do you know yet when you're leaving?"

"I talked to the doctor and he said I could travel by the end of the month. I'm going to do one more concert before I leave, to thank my fans for sticking by me and to say goodbye to them."

"You're not coming back?"

"Maybe someday," she said, "but for now, I'm going to devote myself to my baby. I'm going to spend my time raising him. I want him to be the kind of son that Brad could be proud of, one that will bring honor to his father's name." The tears were rolling down her cheeks. "Oh, Andy, what if I fail that little boy?"

"You won't fail him, Roseanna," Andy said tenderly. "You'll know what to do; it's called mother's instinct. And if you will let me, I'll be there to pinch hit for you in case something comes up that you can't handle."

"Thanks, Andy for offering," she said, "but I don't know, we'll just have to wait and see."

Chapter 13

The concert hall was packed to overflowing. Roseanna had insisted there be no admission fee. She didn't want anyone missing the concert because they couldn't afford a ticket.

Mavis and Kent, Maurice, Sam and Sara had all gone backstage to visit with her. They were sorry to see her leave, but thankful that she had gotten back to the Lord, that her life was at least going in the right direction, and they were thrilled about the baby.

"Why don't you and Andy come out to the ranch after the concert," Mavis suggested. "Maurice and the girls can come and we'll have a going away party for you."

Roseanna gladly accepted the invitation and looked forward to spending her last hours in Nashville with friends.

Travis Houston stepped out on the stage. "Ladies and gentlemen," he said, "we all know why we're here tonight; to bid farewell to a very special lady, and to wish her god-speed. Let's give a great big cheer for Roseanna!"

Roseanna walked out on the stage, her eyes misted with tears.

The crowd stood to its feet. Cheers went up. Applause rang out through the building. Tears rolled down the faces of the audience.

"Thank you," Roseanna said, when they quieted down and took their seats. "I wanted to come here and sing for you tonight, and to thank you for sticking by me through the years, and especially these last few months.

Without all of you, I could not have made it through them. When my husband and little girl were taken from me, I didn't want to live. I came back to the only haven where I felt safe, country music, and you were here waiting. You welcomed me home with open arms. I love all of you and I will never forget you." She wiped the tears that were rolling down her face. "It's time for me to go home now and face the sad memories I left behind. There will also be some happy times ahead. I'm going to have a baby, Brad's baby, a son who will carry on his father's name; Brad will live on through him. I thank God for that. I'm going to try to sing for you, now. Does anyone have a request?

The audience shouted out requests and Roseanna sang their favorite songs for almost two hours. Finally, it came time for the last song of the night. She spoke words from her heart.

"When I lost Brad and Isabelle, I blamed God for taking them from me. I went far from Him. My only refuge, when I wasn't on stage singing, was the bottle. I sank deeper and deeper into the tempest of despair. I could not find my way out. One night I had gone as far as I could go, and I cried out to the Lord for help. His help came in the words of a new song. I didn't want to go there at first, especially when I got to the second verse, because it made me think of Brad and Isabelle, and the way they died, but God showed me He was referring to me. I'm going to sing this song for you, and if there's anyone out there who feels helpless and alone, and you think you can't go any farther on your own, God is there and He will help you." The band started playing the music and through tear-dimmed eyes, Roseanna sang.

"When your road gets long and narrow,
And shadows fall on every side;
When clouds roll in and rain starts falling,

You search through the storm, but there's no place to hide.

There's a door always open and a light always shining,
A fire always burning in a place to call home;
And there's Someone who loves you, who never will leave you,
He's waiting there for you, so, drifter come home.

When the sea gets angry and frightening,
And, lifeboats are useless in waters so strong;
And the wind in your sails takes you too close to danger,
Helpless and hopeless, you're alive but alone.

There's a door always open and a lighthouse that's shining,
A fire always burning in a place to call home;
And there's Someone who loves you, who never will leave you,
He's waiting there for you, so sailor, come home."

She paused. "If you're here tonight and you're being tossed in that tempest, I want to tell you something that my husband told me. I asked him once if he could go through the tempest because he knew that beyond the tempest God was waiting for him. 'Sweetheart,' he said, 'God is not waiting for us beyond the tempest; God is in the tempest with us.' His words came back to me that night, when I was crying out for help, and because of them, and the words of the song God gave me, I realized that God had been there in the tempest with me all along; I just couldn't see Him because of my pain. If there's anyone here tonight who's out in the middle of a tempest of any kind, just know that God is right there with you, wanting to help you; so while I

96

sing the chorus again, give your heart to Him and let Him walk through your tempest with you."

"There's a door always open, and a light always shining,
A fire always burning, in a place to call home;
And there's Someone who loves you who never will leave you,
He's waiting here for you, so drifter come home."

She sang the chorus over and over. She could feel that something was happening; she would never know how many lives she touched that night. But she would find out about two people who were about to make the worst mistakes of their lives until they heard the song.

Jessica, a runaway teenager, down to her last penny, had come inside the concert hall to get the courage to do what she had to do. She had to walk out on that street and sell her body to the first available man. She was scared, but she couldn't survive without food and shelter. The words of the song cut her deep, she knew this was a tempest she was in, and she called on God for help. He answered her prayer, and gave her the courage to call home and talk to her parents. She turned to the young man sitting beside her and told him what happened. "I want to call my parents," she said, "but I don't have the money for the telephone call."

Andy reached in his pocket and pulled out his cell phone. "Call on this," he said smiling.

She dialed the number, and wept when she heard her father's voice. "I love you, Daddy," she cried. "I want to come home, please let me come home."

Andy could hear her father's shout of joy when he heard those words from his little girl. "Of course, you can come home, baby. Your mother and I have been praying for this. We'll wire you the money right away."

"Thank you, Daddy, and tell Mom I love her." She turned to Andy. "Thank you."

"This will tide you over," he said, handing her a big stack of bills.

"How can I repay you," she cried, wiping the tears away.

"You just did," he said, "by making the choice to go back home. And when I tell Roseanna about it, she will be thrilled too."

"You know Roseanna?" she asked in awe.

"Yeah, come with me. I'll introduce you."

Marcie, the mother of three, had decided to end it all. She had the pills in her purse. She was tired of the rat race. She had not been able to cope with all the stress and responsibilities that had been thrust upon her when her husband walked out on his family. Her kids would be better off without her; their grandparents would make sure they were loved and cared for. She had brought them to this concert because they loved Roseanna. She wanted to do this one last thing for them. She would drop them off at her parent's house, afterward, to spend the weekend, then, she would go home and end it all. As Roseanna sang the song, she could see God with her, here in this tempest that was pulling her under. "Oh, God, help me," she prayed and hope was renewed within her. She scribbled a note, telling all about what she had intended to do, and the decision she'd made when she heard the song. "Give this to Roseanna," she said, handing the note to an usher. She watched as he handed it to her. Roseanna looked back at her, nodded her head and smiled. Marcie went home that night, washed the pills down the drain, got on her knees and thanked God for her life.

Chapter 14

"Roseanna, do you feel okay?" Andy asked for the hundredth time since starting on the long trip home to the bayou. The doctor had said she'd have to be careful, and he wasn't taking any chances. "Do we need to stop?"

"Not now," she said, "but I do want to make an extra stop before we get home. I want to go by Brad's parents in Mississippi. It's not much out of the way and I really want to see them."

"Just tell me which exit to take," he said, a little apprehensive at going any extra miles. Roseanna was tired; he could see it in her face. She'd put her all into the concert last night, then the party afterwards. And they'd left out early this morning so there hadn't been much time for sleep. "Did you get any sleep at all last night?" he asked.

"Not much, I was too excited to sleep. Don't worry Andy, I'm okay," she said.

It was late afternoon when they pulled into the yard of Brad's parents home.

"I'll stay in the car while you go in," Andy said, understanding that she needed time alone with them.

"Thank you, Andy," she said, gratefully.

"Roseanna," Janet Lefourche exclaimed happily when she opened the door.

"Mom, it's so good to see you," Roseanna said, embracing her warmly. "Is Dad around?"

"He's out tending the cattle, he should be back any minute, now." She had barely gotten the words out when he walked in the back door.

"Whose car is that out front?" he asked, walking into the living room. "Roseanna," he cried joyfully, seeing her standing there.

She ran into his arms and wept. "Dad, I've missed you both so much."

"And, we've missed you, daughter," he said, holding her close. "We've been so worried about you."

"I know, and I'm sorry," she said. "I've been so messed up. I stayed away from my family and friends because of the memories of Brad and Isabelle. Please forgive me for neglecting you." She was crying as she held on to them.

"Honey, there's nothing to forgive," her mother-in-law said. "We know how hard losing them is on you; it's hard on us, but at least we still have each other; you were left without anyone. My precious child, I don't how you survived."

They wept together over the loss of Brad and Isabelle. They shared memories that were precious to them, and cried some more. Roseanna shared all the latest news about the baby with them.

"I'm going to name him William Bradley and call him Will," she told them, a sparkle in her eye. "He couldn't have two better namesakes."

"This baby is indeed a miracle," Janet said. "I never dreamed I would ever hold another grandchild in my arms, and God has given us a boy. He won't take Brad's place of course, but he will make losing him a little more bearable."

William Lefouche took his wife in his arms. Tears were running down his face. "We've got something to be thankful for," he whispered.

"Will you spend the night?" Janet asked, composing herself somewhat and remembering her manners.

"I'm not sure yet," Roseanna said. "I'm not alone. A friend is driving me home and he's waiting in the car."

"Invite him in," her father-in-law said, starting for the door.

"Wait," Roseanna said, "there's something I want to tell you before he comes in. She told them the whole story; how lonely and empty her life was without Brad and Isabelle; about the terrible nightmares; how she had started drinking to try to blot out the horrible visions of them being in the water, and of their voices crying out to her to help them. "I was at my wits end when God sent this young man to help me." She told them about Andy and what a dear friend he had become and how he had brought some happiness into her life, and was helping her deal with her loss. "There's something else I need to tell you," she said, reaching out for the right words to say. "He has asked me to marry him. He knows I don't love him in the way a wife should love her husband. I can only love Brad that way. He will always be my only true husband. Andy knows this but he wants to marry me anyway. He wants to take care of me, and the baby. Of course, my son will always have his daddy's name, he will always be a Lefourche; I would never take that from him, or Brad, or you. I haven't given Andy my final answer; but I've told him I don't think I can ever marry another man, even if it is in name only. I wanted to talk this over with you, and tell you that if I do decide to marry him, you will still be my family, and I hope I will always be a part of yours."

"Of course you will," Brad's father said. "You're our daughter and will always be welcome in our home, no matter what your last name is. We want you to be happy; and if this young man makes you happy, then we'll accept him in our family too. Now, get him in here so we can meet him."

Andy and Brad's parents hit it off immediately. He liked the warm friendliness they extended to him. They liked the easy way he had about him, the way he came through as being honest and forthright.

"Roseanna, honey, you look tired, maybe you'd better spend the night here with us," Janet suggested.

"Yeah, I don't think she needs to travel any more today," Andy said. "I can get a room in a hotel…"

"Nonsense," Brad's father said. "We have an extra guest room, you can stay right here."

"Thank you sir, I'd like that," Andy replied.

"I'll get supper started," Janet said, heading for the kitchen.

Roseanna stood up to go help her.

"You stay put, young lady," Andy told her. "I'll go help with supper. As you know, I'm pretty handy in the kitchen."

Roseanna smiled. Andy was fitting right in. She could hear him and Janet talking and laughing as they prepared supper. And what a meal it was. Meatloaf, mashed potatoes, green beans, canned from Janet Lefourche's garden, corn, also from the garden, and her special lemon cream pie.

"Mom, this is delicious," Roseanna said, as she passed her plate for seconds.

Janet smiled. "Thank you, dear. It's good to see you eating again."

Andy stood and took a bow. "Thank you. Thank you. I had a hand in preparing this feast," he said, causing them to laugh. Laughter was needed in this house; it had been too long since there had been anything to laugh about.

After supper was finished and the kitchen cleaned up, they sat around looking at old pictures of Brad when he was a boy, reliving the precious memories his Mom and Dad had of him. It was hard on Roseanna to see the pictures, and hear the stories about him, but she didn't let it show. It was important to his parents to talk about him; to remember; to share their memories.

Roseanna dreaded going to bed. She would be sleeping in Brad's old room, surrounded by things from his childhood that he had held dear. All his memoirs were there, some of his clothes still in the closet.

"Sweetheart," Janet said, putting her arm around Roseanna, "would you like to sleep in the guest room?"

Roseanna hugged her. "Thank you, Mom, for understanding."

"I can't go back in his room, yet, and I know it would be hard on you," she said. "We'll put Andy in Brad's room."

It was hard saying goodbye the next morning. Roseanna clung to them. "I feel close to Brad when I'm here with you," she said, as tears ran down her cheeks.

"Come back, soon," they said, waving to her as the car pulled out of the driveway and out onto the highway.

Roseanna waved until they vanished from sight; then she broke down and wept. "I've neglected them shamefully," she cried. "I've got to come visit them more often."

"We'll come back often," Andy promised.

"*We'll* come back," Roseanna mused to herself. Was he so sure that he would always be a part of her life?

The sun was going down behind the horizon when Roseanna and Andy finally pulled into Grandma's yard. The whole family was waiting. They rushed to the car, and not waiting for Roseanna to get out, they all grabbed her at once. Amid hugs and kisses, tears and shouts of joy, they made their way inside. Everyone was talking at once and no one understood what anyone was saying, but that didn't matter; Roseanna was home; and that's what mattered.

"This is Andy Winslow, a good friend of mine," Roseanna said, when the noise died down enough for her to be heard.

They gathered around him, shaking his hand and mumbling the usual amenities.

Belle held on to Roseanna. "Sis, I was so worried about you," she said, tears streaming down her face. "I'm never going to let go of you again."

"I'm okay, now, Belle, don't worry," Roseanna said, hugging her sister tightly. "I'm still hurting over losing Brad and Isabelle, I always will; but I am able to cope now, since I turned things over to the Lord; and Andy has helped me, too."

"I've got to hear more about Andy," Belle whispered, not wanting him to overhear.

"We sneak away by ourselves later and I'll tell you everything," Roseanna promised. "But now, we'd better go join the others."

"Grandma, this is wonderful stuff, whatever it is," Andy remarked, taking a bite of gumbo for the first time.

Grandma beamed as she always did when someone bragged on her cooking.

They had a wonderful time, talking and laughing, and eating their fill of Grandma's gumbo. Roseanna stole a glance at Andy. He was having a good time. He fit in here, too. He had won Grandma's favor and that meant a lot.

The evening wore on and it was time for everyone to say goodnight. It was hard for Roseanna to say goodbye to them, even for a few hours. She wanted to hold on to all of them. They tried to convince her to spend the night with some of the family, but she wanted to go home. She had to face the memories there, and she didn't want to put it off.

Andy drove her to the parsonage and took her luggage inside.

"Are you really sure you want to stay here?" he asked, solemnly.

"I've got to," she told him.

"Then, I'm staying too," he said.

"No," I've got to do this by myself," she said firmly. "I want to be here alone with Brad and Isabelle."

"I'll only be a couple of minutes away," he told her. "If you need me, call me on my cell phone and I'll be here in a jiffy."

"Okay," she said, "thanks."

"I'll go, and let you get some rest," he said. "Is there anything I can do before I leave?"

She shook her head. "I'll call if I need you, I promise."

After he left, she looked around the room at the familiar things that had meant so much to Brad and her. She rubbed her hand over the back of his chair, where he spent so much time reading his Bible and studying his sermons. Tears ran down her face as memories flooded through her. It was if she could see him sitting there, Bible in his hand, and her sitting on the arm of the chair, with her head resting on his shoulder. He liked having her close by; he said he could study much better with her there by his side. "Oh, Brad," she cried out, "I miss you so much, baby."

She forced herself to walk into Isabelle's room. A cry of pain came from her lips as she saw all of her daughter's things. She ran her hand over the dolls and stuffed animals on the bed. She'd have to put Pooh Bear back in his place with the other toys. She picked up a picture of Isabelle, and wept as she longed to hold her baby again, to tuck her in and hear her prayers. She gasped for breath as her throat closed up from the pain going through her. She ran out of the room.

She stood motionless, before the door that led to the other bedroom, the room she had shared with Brad. Could she go in there? Her legs were like lead. They refused to move. "I've got to go in there," she muttered and forced her legs to take her forward.

Waves of loneliness and pangs of agony swept over her as she stepped into the room. Brad's stuff was still where he'd left it. She picked his Bible up from off the nightstand. His favorite scripture, Psalms 91, was marked with a bookmark that Isabelle had made for him in Vacation Bible School. She tried to read the verses, but her eyes were filled with tears and the words ran together.

Wiping away the tears as best she could, she walked over to the closet. Brad's clothes were hanging there, neatly arranged by color combinations. He was so well organized, and much neater then her. She took one of the shirts off the hanger and held it close. She rubbed her face against the fabric. Her heart almost burst within her with longing for him. "Brad, what am I going to do without you and Isabelle? Time passes, but the hurt doesn't get any less. I love you, my darling; I'll always love you. Remember how we always said we were each other's past, present, and future. All I have left is the past, cause the present is too painful, and the future doesn't exist for me without you and Isabelle, except through our son. He'll be born in a few weeks." Tears were rolling down her face now. "Oh, Brad, I thank God for him; through this child I will have a little part of you to hold on to. I'm going to cherish that little boy. I'm going to make sure that he knows you and Isabelle; that you both will always be a big part of his life as you are in mine. I wish you could be here to hold him. I wish he could walk through life holding on to your hand, with your strength and wisdom to guide him. Oh, Brad, please look down and help me raise our son, I'm not sure I can do it alone."

As she stood there, she thought of Andy's proposal. Dear, sweet Andy, willing to put his life on hold to marry her and help raise her son, even though he knew she didn't love him and could never be a real wife to him. Could she let him accept second best just to be there for her? And what about her, could she marry someone else and share their name? Her heart cried out to Brad for help.

"Oh, Brad, how can I marry him when in my heart I'm still married to you, and I always will be. I'm not in love with him, sweetheart, for I could never love anyone but you; but he does make me happy, and without him around my life is empty and bleak. Brad, I don't want to give up your name; I want to always be Mrs. Bradley Lefourche, but I'm so lost and lonely. Please tell me what to do, Brad. Please help me know what's right." But the answer didn't come; instead feelings of desperation seized her. She fell down across the bed, sobbing and screaming out in pain. Anguish swept through her, her insides felt like they were on fire. It was like she was being torn apart at the seams. She grabbed the cell phone and dialed.

Andy was there in a matter of minutes. He ran into the house. He rushed to Roseanna's side.

She fell into his arms. "Hold me," she cried, "please hold me. Don't ever let go of me."

He pulled her close and held her tenderly. "I'll always be here," he whispered, wiping away her tears. He wished he could take her pain away, but he couldn't, all he could do was hold her and try to comfort her.

"I want to go to the ocean," she said, after she composed herself a bit. "I want to be near Brad and Isabelle. Please take me to the ocean."

"Roseanna, it's too far away. You can't travel all the way to Florida," he reminded her, "not until after the baby is born."

"I'm not talking about going to Florida," she explained. "The ocean is not far from here. That's where I want to go; please say you'll take me."

"Sure," he said, "we'll go first thing tomorrow."

"I want to go now."

"You need to rest…"

"I can't rest, not until I…go there."

He finally gave in and soon they were in his car on their way. He parked in a secluded spot along the beach and they got out. They climbed up on a huge rock that overlooked the ocean. The moonlight gave just enough light for them to find their way safely to the top of the rock. They stood there looking out over the waters, listening to the waves as they lapped gently against the rocks.

"I wonder where they are out there," Roseanna reflected, as tears streamed down her face. "Where is Brad? Where is my baby? Did Brad reach our Isabelle or did they each die alone? How scared Isabelle must have been, in those raging waters all alone; and the terror Brad must have felt if he couldn't reach her…" She was sobbing uncontrollably. "Oh, God," she cried out in anguish as the horror of what happened crushed her heart within her.

Andy took her in his arms but he didn't try to quiet her. He knew she had to get this out, as painful as it was; she had to deal with it.

"Andy," she cried, "I kissed them goodbye that morning and I never saw them again, not even in death. They're gone, and there's nothing of them left here. There were no goodbyes; there's no grave for me to visit; if I could see them and kiss them goodbye, if I could just tell them how much I love and miss them; if I could just put flowers on their graves…"

"Come go with me," he said. "The shops along the beach stay open late. I feel certain we can find what we need."

They returned to the beach a little while later loaded down with pink and yellow roses. Roseanna had bought every pink and yellow rose in the store.

Roseanna," Andy said gently, holding on to her, "this is Brad and Isabelle's final resting place, it's their grave, and you can overlay their graves with flowers. You can't see their faces or kiss them goodbye, but you can talk to them, you can tell them how much you love them and miss them. I'll go so you can have this time alone with them. I'll be in the car."

"Andy, please don't go," she said, with a pleading look in her eyes. "I need you here with me. I can't say goodbye to them without you beside me." She dropped a pink rose into the water. "My sweet Isabelle, this pink rose is for you. Pink is your favorite color and you will be covered in a cascade of pink." Tears blinded her as she picked up all the pink roses and dropped them in the water. "Go find the spot where my baby is buried and cover her with your beauty and sweet fragrance." She cried as her heart broke inside her. "Isabelle, my precious, I miss you so much. I will never understand why you had to be taken from me. Mommy will always love you, my angel girl; and I will cherish the memories of you that I hold in my heart. Goodbye, until I see you again."

She picked up the yellow roses. "Brad, yellow roses adorned the church the day you and I became man and wife. I send these yellow roses to you, my beloved husband, in honor of that day, and the love we will always share." She sang in sweet tones some of the love song she sang to him at their wedding.

"Like apples of gold in pitchers of silver,
Like raindrops that turn into rivers of wine;

109

Like a soft wind moves cross a high green meadow,
Like a ruby that glows, babe, like a diamond that
shines;
Like a candle that burns with a slow certain passion,
Like the call of a dove from a tall oak tree;
Like cherries in bloom at the end of December,
You belong in my heart, babe…."

Tears streamed down her face as she went back in memory to the day she stood before the altar, and pledged herself to Brad forever. "Brad, I still love you as much as I did when I first sang those words to you. I will always love you, but I've got to say goodbye to you, now, and it tears my heart out. It won't be goodbye forever, sweetheart; I will see you again, and our love will go on, throughout all eternity. Keep watching for me, and one day I will come home to Isabelle and you. I love you, Brad. I love you Isabelle. Goodbye my darlings." She turned, and fell into Andy's arms, grieving for the loves she'd lost and the finality of goodbye.

Chapter 15

Six months earlier, on an island somewhere out in the Atlantic Ocean, a man lay sprawled on the beach. He looked more dead than alive. On the brink of consciousness, his inner being sought for release. Darkness swirled around him as he was hurled back and forth in the turbulence that encompassed him. His eyelids fluttered. He opened his eyes. Where was he? What happened? He shook his head, trying to get his bearings. Then he remembered. Panic seized him.

"Isabelle," he cried out, fear pounding like a giant drum in his chest.

"Daddy."

He turned and saw her lying there in the white sand beside him. A cry of relief came from his lips. He grabbed her and pulled her close. "My baby," he whispered. "My Isabelle. Are you all right?" He kissed her again and again.

She clung to him. "I'm scared, Daddy, hold me," she cried.

"Daddy's here, baby," he said, tears of joy flowing down his face, as he held her trembling body in his arms. "Don't be afraid."

"Daddy, the water's so cold and dark," she cried again. "I'm scared,"

"You're not in the water now, sweetheart," he said, cupping her face in his hands and looking down at her. "You're safe."

"Where are we Daddy?"

He looked around. "We seem to be on an island, I'm not sure where," he said.

"I want to go home, Daddy," she cried. "I want Mommy."

He held her close. "I want Mommy too, sweetheart." His voice choked as he thought of his beloved Roseanna, and realized what she must be going through.

"Does Mommy know where we are?" Isabelle asked. "Will she come get us?"

"No, sweetheart, Mommy doesn't know where we are..."

"Are we lost, Daddy?" she cried out.

"To some people we're lost, but God knows exactly where we are. He's looking at us right now."

Isabelle looked up to the sky. "God, please tell Mommy where we are so she can come get us."

Brad winched. How could he make Isabelle understand that God would not do what she had just asked Him to do; he had always taught her that God could do anything; how can he explain this to her, without taking away her childlike faith.

"Honey, listen to Daddy," he said tenderly, "even though God knows where we are, other folks will have to find us. God will watch over us and He will take care of us..."

"Why won't He tell someone where we are, Daddy, so they can come and get us?"

He pondered a moment. He didn't know exactly how to answer her question. "There are some things that God does Himself, and then there are some things that He puts people in charge of," he said thoughtfully, "and this is one of those things that people have to do."

"How long 'til the people find us?" she asked tearfully.

"I don't know, sweetheart," he told her truthfully. "I hope it will be soon."

"How did we get here, Daddy?"

"Baby, I don't know how we got here," he said, his mind reliving the horrible ordeal. He remembered the terror he felt when he saw Isabelle fall over the side of the boat; jumping in after her, grabbing hold of her, and holding on even though the raging waters tore at them and swept them away so fast that he couldn't fight against the fury. He remembered a log floating by, and, grabbing hold of it. He remembered holding on to Isabelle with one arm and on to the log with the other. He remembered fighting for hours to stay afloat ---being so tired, feeling himself slipping---then nothing, 'til he woke up, here. "What do you remember, Isabelle?"

"I fell in the water. I was really scared, then you were there, you had hold of me, and the water was making us go so fast, we went under the water, and it was dark, then we were holding on to a log and we held on for a long time, then you turned loose and we went under again, it was dark and scary; then you picked me up in your hands and lifted me out of the water. Daddy your hands were so big..."

"What happened then?" Brad asked anxiously, realizing that Isabelle had witnessed a wonderful miracle.

"I fell asleep, I don't remember anything else," she said. "Did you bring us here in your big hands, Daddy?"

"Sweetheart, those weren't my hands that got you out of the water; those were God's hands; He got me out too, and He brought us here, to safety. We need to thank Him for rescuing us."

"Thank You, God, for getting Daddy and me out of the water," Isabelle prayed in childlike tones. "Now, God, please take us back to Mommy."

Brad prayed over the lump in his throat. "Thank You, Father, for watching over Isabelle and me, and rescuing us. Now, Father, I ask You to watch over my precious Roseanna; take care of her, Lord..." Tears were streaming down his face as he thought of the unbearable pain that Roseanna was going through.

"Is Mommy sad, Daddy?"

"Yes, baby, Mommy is very sad," he answered, taking his little girl in his arms. "We'll have to pray for Mommy everyday until we get back home to her."

"I want to go home, now, Daddy. I want Mommy."

"I know, sweetheart," he said, kissing her on the cheek, "but we may not get to go home right away. We've got to be brave. Let's count this as a big adventure; one where we will have to find our way back to Mommy, and while we're waiting to get back home, we'll look for ways to survive here." Isabelle loved adventures, and he hoped this would keep her from being afraid while they were waiting to be rescued. He checked his pocket. His billfold was still there. "Thank goodness," he muttered. The money was soaked, but still intact. He took it out and laid it in the warm sunshine to dry.

"What do we do first, Daddy?" she asked with a twinge of excitement in her voice.

"First, we look for food," he said, taking her hand. "We'll walk around the island and see what we can find to eat."

"Are there any bears on the island?" she asked, her eyes big with fear, as she pressed close to him.

"I don't think so," he said, trying to put her mind at ease. His knowledge of islands was very limited, but he didn't think bears lived on islands out here in the ocean, at least he hoped they didn't; but she had posed a serious question; were there dangerous animals on the island, and, if so, how would he protect Isabelle and himself from them?

"Daddy, look at the pretty flowers," she exclaimed as a cascade of red, purple, pink and blue flowers greeted them as they walked through the foliage, looking for any thing that was edible. They found a fig tree and some wild onions.

"This will be enough for today," Brad said, noticing that the sun was getting low on the horizon, and not wanting to be out here when darkness came. He felt safer, on the sandy beach, where he could at least see anything that might be coming toward them.

They sat down on the beach to eat. The figs tasted good, but Isabelle gagged when she tried to eat the onions. Brad, realizing they might be here a long time and have to survive on such foods, had to find a way to get her to eat them, so he decided to go forward with the adventure theme.

"We're like two trailblazers, forging out new horizons," he said, "having to scrounge around for food and shelter; living off whatever we can scrape together..."

"We're not going to have much to eat, are we, Daddy?"

He marveled at the wisdom Isabelle showed, how quickly she had figured things out. "No, we probably won't have a lot to eat," he said, "but we will have enough. God is watching over us, and he will send us enough to eat, even if He has to rain manna down from heaven again, or send food to us by a raven.

"What's manna, and how can a bird feed us? she asked inquisitively.

"I'll tell you all about it," he said, pulling her into his lap. She snuggled close to him. "This will be a bedtime story," he added, noticing the big yawn that she could not suppress. By the time he finished, she was rubbing her eyes sleepily. "Sleep tight, little one," he said, giving her a good night kiss.

As he sat there in the darkness, holding on to her, he felt an eerie presence, like someone watching them. A chill ran up his spine. Was something or someone out there watching their every move? If someone else was here, what kind of person or persons were they? Did they intend to do them harm? If they were friendly, why hadn't they shown themselves? Why were they hiding in the shadows? "I'll stay awake and watch over Isabelle, tonight," he purposed, but even now his eyelids were getting heavy and he felt sleep falling on him. He realized how totally helpless he was, so he went to the Source of all his help.

"Father, our lives are in your Hands. I can't do anything to protect Isabelle or myself, but You can. I don't see a way out of this, but You do. You saved us from drowning. You can protect us now, and supply our needs. Watch over us, and watch over Roseanna. Keep her safe in your care, and make a way for us to get home to her." He fought the drowsiness that was coming over him, but eventually he lost the battle and drifted off to sleep, holding Isabelle snugly in his arms.

Chapter 16

"Daddy! Daddy! Wake up!" Isabelle yelled, shaking him excitedly. "God did it! He rained all this stuff down from heaven!"

Brad sat upright. He rubbed his eyes to make sure he wasn't seeing things. Lying at the edge of the clearing was a big box. He hurried over to it and looked inside. There were canned goods of all kinds, a can opener, some pots and pans, two metal plates and mugs, forks and spoons, a sharp knife, several gallon jugs of water, a big box of matches, a package of razors, some soap, a fishing pole and two sleeping bags.

"Do they have sleeping bags and fishing poles in heaven, Daddy?" Isabelle asked, her eyes wide with wonder.

"I didn't think so," he told her.

"Did God make these specially for us?"

"It would seem so," he said, looking around for tracks. God had certainly supplied the provisions, but He had done it through human hands. Who else was here on the island? What were they planning? If they meant to do them harm, why had they brought these things? He'd try to find out later. Right now, Isabelle was hungry. "Baby, what would you like to eat?"

She looked through the canned goods and picked out two. Vienna sausage and sliced peaches didn't top the list of his favorite breakfast foods, but compared to what they ate yesterday, it was a gourmet meal.

Isabelle was excited. "We won't have to eat any more onions," she said, smiling.

Brad didn't have the heart to tell her that these supplies wouldn't last forever. If they weren't rescued from the island soon, would the unknown benefactor come back with more food, or would they have to go back to fruit and wild onions?

When they finished eating, he washed the dishes in the shallow water that ran up to the beach, then, they started on a tour of the island. As they walked along, he looked for signs of life; but found none. Someone else had to be here, but where? And why were they hiding? Why did they not want to be found? Why would anyone hide away in a place like this, cut off from society completely? Brad could think of only one reason; and it scared him.

"Let's get back to camp, honey," he said, not wanting to get too far away for fear of getting lost.

"Okay," she said, a bit reluctantly. She liked scouting the island, finding new adventures, smelling the pretty flowers.

"Let's try out that fishing pole and see if we can catch our supper," Brad suggested, seeing her disappointment. "I'll teach you how to fish."

"Okay," she squealed. "I'll catch lots of fish, Daddy, you'll see."

Brad dug the worms and they waded out into the water. He cast the pole and let Isabelle help him reel it in. After several tries, they finally caught a good size fish, and two smaller ones. "This will be enough for supper," he said.

"Let's fish some more," she pleaded.

"We only need as many as we can eat," he explained. "We'll fish again tomorrow."

He built a fire late that afternoon and cooked their catch. They sat around the fire, eating until the last bite of fish had vanished.

"That was good, Daddy," Isabelle said. "We catch the best fish in the world, don't we?"

118

"You bet we do," he said, thankful that she was happy, at least for a little while.

A week passed. Brad had not seen even an inkling of a ship on the horizon, no airplanes overhead searching for them. Had they called off the search already? Roseanna would never give up on them; she'd know in her heart they were still alive and she would search 'til she found them. But that might take forever. He needed to find a way off the island, but how? If he were alone, maybe he could swim in search of help; but he couldn't chance it with Isabelle. He wouldn't put her back out in that water, and he couldn't leave her here alone. How far were they from civilization, from home?

"Oh, my sweet Roseanna," he cried as he felt the intensity of her pain. He wanted to go to her, as he had done so many times before when she needed him; but this time he couldn't get to her. He couldn't hold her in his arms and kiss her 'til the pain went away. She would have to face this without him. How totally devastated she had to be, thinking that she had lost both Isabelle and him. Her words rang in his ears; 'Brad, don't ever leave me again. I can't survive without you, can't survive without you, can't survive…' His heart broke within him. "Oh, God, please help her," he cried.

That night as he sat watching Isabelle sleeping peacefully in her sleeping bag, his thoughts ran rampant. The mysterious stranger had not visited them again; but Brad had sensed his presence, lurking in the darkness, watching them. Why did he only come out at night? What did he have on his mind? Was he waiting to get Isabelle alone, away from Brad's watchful eye? The thought terrified him. "I won't let her out of my sight," he purposed silently. But what about at night when they were sleeping; could the stranger slip in and take her right out from under his nose? He pulled his sleeping bag over next to Isabelle's, and put his arms tightly around her. No one could take her out of his grasp without waking him up.

Isabelle woke up the next morning, crying for Roseanna. "Mommy! Mommy!" she cried. "I want to go home. I want Mommy!"

Brad pulled his daughter close and dried her tears. It broke his heart to see her suffer this way. "Why, God?" he cried. "Why did this happen? Is there a purpose to all this?" His faith in God had not been dampened, but he didn't know why his precious wife and daughter had to suffer this way. His heart cried out for understanding. His arms ached to hold Roseanna. Tears slid down his face as he thought of the unbearable pain she was in. "Why, God, why?" he cried again.

Another week passed. Brad kept count of the days by making marks in the sand. He looked at Isabelle. How would this ordeal affect her? What if they were stranded here for months, years? Would Roseanna eventually give up hope that they were still alive, and what would it do to her when she had let go of them? He knew the answer, and it scared him more than being stranded on this island. His precious Roseanna couldn't survive, she wasn't strong enough. She had always leaned on him for strength; and he had let her. It made him feel good that she depended so much on him; that he could always be there to make things right for her. Now he realized what a mistake that was. He should have helped her find strength to trust in God for herself. "What have I done?" he cried in despair, as he thought of Roseanna there alone without the faith she needed to reach out to God for help. "Sweetheart, I've failed you," he whispered, his heart breaking inside him. "God, please help her to find that strength."

He had helped make a spiritual cripple out of her, one that needed him as a crutch to help her stand. He had to get home to her, but how?

With all the new technology out today, they'd be able to find them, Brad reasoned; but would they? He had no idea how far the surging waters had carried them, or, where God had set them down. They could be hundreds of miles from where they went into the water. Suddenly it all seemed hopeless, and for the first time, his faith wavered.

"Daddy, does God know we don't have much food left," Isabelle questioned, frowning, as she thought of the wild onions.

"Yes baby, God knows all about us, and He's going to take care of us." Just reassuring his daughter that everything would be okay restored his complete trust in God. "Thy will be done," he whispered as he put their fate and future in the Father's hands.

Chapter 17

Brad lay awake staring into the darkness. He had to make plans for Isabelle's immediate future, the days ahead that they would spend here on this island. It wasn't enough that she survive; she had to live as much a normal life as possible under the circumstances. She had to be a little girl and do the things that a little girl would do. She had to learn the things that she would be learning now if she were back home in school. She had to play like she would play at home, without the benefit of her toys and games. Just making sure she was fed and protected wasn't enough; she had to be nurtured. Roseanna had always taken care of the nurturing part; but now he had to do it. He had to be a father, a mother, a teacher, a spiritual leader, and, yes, even a playmate to his daughter, for all these things were important to her development. When they got back home, (and he was sure they would someday,) he wanted her to be emotionally stable as well as physically strong. He didn't want her to fall behind in her education; but how could he teach her without the proper supplies? "Lord, help me find a way," he prayed, before dropping off to sleep.

The next morning he frowned as he noticed how low their food supply had become. He couldn't rely on the stranger to bring them more, and he had to make sure Isabelle had plenty to eat. "It doesn't take much for me to survive," he uttered, under his breath. He fixed half the amount of food for breakfast as he usually did, and he only ate a few bites. He would do the same for the other meals.

That way the food would last longer and Isabelle would have plenty to eat. He could live on the fish they caught, and he could eat the wild onions.

After they finished breakfast, he called Isabelle over to him. "We're going to play school," he said, making a game out of it so she wouldn't suspect what he was really up to. "First, we'll do reading."

"Daddy, we don't have any books," she pointed out, "how are we going to have school?"

He picked up the sharp stick that he had used to mark the days off. "I'll write some words here in the sand and teach you to read them," he said, searching his memory for Bible verses that were not too difficult for a six year old to read.

"God is love," he wrote in the sand, then read the words to her.

"Daddy, that's easy," she said. "I already know how to read that."

"Of course," he said, realizing she didn't really know the words, but she knew the verse, she had memorized it in church. He had to figure out another way to teach her the words. He mixed the words up and wrote them in the sand. He pointed to the first word. "Can you read that?"

She shook her head.

"Love, that word is love," he told her, going over each word until she could read it by herself; then he had her write them in the sand. "School's out for today," he said, after an hour or so, not wanting to tire her out the first day. "Lets go for a swim."

The water was warm and inviting. They swam and played for the rest of the morning, splashing water on each other, and racing to the reef that was the border line Brad had set for her. She was never to go farther into the water than the reef.

123

He opened a can of Vienna sausage for lunch. "You eat all of them," he told her. "I'm not very hungry and I want to have plenty of room for all those fish we're going to catch for supper tonight."

After lunch, he came up with an idea. "Let's gather lots of these vines," he said, making sure they were not poison ivy. "We're going to make a couple of jump ropes. One for you and one for me."

"Can you jump rope, Daddy?"

He laughed. "We'll soon find out."

They worked all afternoon weaving the heavy vines together in two long lengths. It was late when they finished the jump ropes. There was no time to go fishing, so Brad opened a can of soup for supper. He built a fire and warmed it up. He filled Isabelle's plate up to the brim and poured the rest for himself.

"Daddy, your plate doesn't have much in it," she said. "You want some of mine?"

"No, thank you, honey, I have plenty, " he assured her.

After supper, they had a rope-jumping contest. Isabelle giggled when Brad tried to jump 'red hot pepper'. "That's not the way you do it, Daddy," she said.

"I guess I'm a little out of practice," he replied, laughing it off.

They were both ready for bed by the time the contest was over. Isabelle had won thumbs down. "Maybe, you'll do better tomorrow," she said, giving him a goodnight kiss.

Just then the sound of a gunshot ripped through the quietness of the night. Brad pushed Isabelle to the ground and shielded her with his body. "Don't move," he whispered, panic going through every nerve of his body. An eerie stillness followed. Would the next shot be for them? They lay there for what seemed like an eternity. "I think it's okay, now," he told Isabelle, helping her to her feet.

"Daddy, what was that noise?"

He didn't want to scare her, but he couldn't lie. "Baby, it sounded like a gun shot."

"Does God shoot guns?"

"I've never known Him to, but He does watch over little girls. Don't be afraid, you're safe now," Brad said, trying to reassure her.

"I'm not afraid. I've got you and God watching over me," she said, trying to stifle a yawn. "I'm going to bed now."

Brad's heart was troubled as he helped his daughter into bed. His suspicions were confirmed; there was someone else on the island and that person had a gun. How could he go up against someone with a gun? What chance did he have of protecting himself and Isabelle?

Brad looked at his daughter, already sleeping peacefully; he marveled at her faith. She could lay down and sleep because God was watching over her. Oh, if only he could grasp that kind of faith. He *knew* God was watching over them; but he still couldn't relax; he'd stay awake all night, and watch, in case the man with the gun tried to come into their camp.

As he sat there, trying to watch in every direction, an incident from his past flashed through his mind. He hadn't thought of it in years. It happened when he was a young boy. There was this kid; Kenny was his name, and he lived on the neighboring farm. He was a little older than Brad, but twice his size. Brad always suspected that Kenny came from a family of giants. They would play together, even though the boy was a bully and enjoyed bossing him around. Kenny had this pocket knife, and if Brad didn't do everything he told him to, he would threaten to cut his head off. Brad, being smaller than Kenny and not very brave, did whatever he was told to do. They played the games Kenny wanted to play, the way Kenny wanted to play them.

Brad shared all his treats and toys with Kenny; Kenny shared none of his with Brad.

Why did God bring this memory to him? Was He trying to remind Brad what a coward he was back then? "I already know that, God," he mumbled. Then his mind went ahead to how it all played out.

They were playing cowboys at Kenny's house and built a jail out of some long planks, they had to have a prisoner to go in their jail, so they arrested Kenny's mother's favorite cat. One of the planks fell over and killed the cat. He and Kenny hid behind the smokehouse and saw what happened next. Kenny's little brother walked by and found the cat right before the mother came walking up. She saw the cat, and Kenny's brother there at the scene, and concluded that he had killed her cat. What happened to him wasn't pleasant to watch.

Brad smiled. "God, I know what You're trying to show me now," he said, as memories of what happened next flashed through his mind.

Kenny looked at him with a 'please don't tell' look in his eye. From that day on, he never threatened Brad again, they played the games Brad wanted to play, the way he wanted to play them. Kenny shared his toys and treats with Brad. Brad's life took a gigantic turn for the good. What made the difference? Brad had got him an equalizer. The secret he knew made him equal with the bigger boy, he no longer had to fear what he might do to him.

Brad nodded his head with understanding. "That man out there has a gun and I'm no equal to that; but I have You on my side, God, and that puts the odds in my favor; You are my Equalizer, so I no longer have to fear what that man can do to us, for my Equalizer will take care of him, if he tries to harm us." He smiled and laid down. "Thank You, God," he said drifting off to a peaceful sleep.

Chapter 18

"Daddy, wake up, Daddy," Isabelle urged, shaking him. But he didn't stir. "Daddy, please wake up," she said again, her lips trembling.

Two more weeks had passed, and Brad had continued to eat only a few bites at each meal in order that Isabelle would have plenty to eat. He had felt a weakness coming over him for a couple of days, but had ignored it in order to take care of her. He'd gone to sleep last night feeling nauseous and a little disoriented, not really concerned, thinking he'd be okay after a good nights sleep.

"Daddy, you're so hot," Isabelle cried, touching his face. She shook him harder, "Daddy, wake up." But he didn't. She was afraid. She had to get help. He'd told her never to go off by herself; but now he was sick; and sick people died. Was he going to die? Her heart pounded in fear. "I've got to find God," she whispered and ran, stumbling across the island. She tripped on the vines, and sharp leaves scratched her arms and face, but she kept going. She had to find God. She had heard his footsteps in the darkness so she knew He was here, and He'd know what to do.

She saw someone standing in a clearing. She ran to him and tugged at his sleeve. "Are you God," she asked with the innocence of a child.

The man standing there jumped with surprise and started to run away.

"No, God, please don't go," she pleaded, tears streaming down her face. "My daddy's sick. He needs You."

The man spoke without turning to face her. "Kid, I'm not God, and I can't help your daddy." His voice was harsh, unfeeling. "Now, go away and leave me alone."

"No, you've got to help him," she said, determinedly. "He's gonna die. Please, mister, help him, please, don't let my daddy die." She tugged at the man's sleeve harder.

The man pulled away. "Leave me alone!" he snapped. "I'm not God, and I can't help your daddy."

Isabelle started to cry. "Please, mister, please," she begged.

"Go away, kid," he said, a little less gruffly.

Isabelle stood her ground. "No, I won't go away!" she yelled between sobs. "My daddy is all I've got left, and he's real sick. I love my daddy; you got to help us, Mister. Please. Please," she begged again.

The big man standing there brushed away the tear that was trying to run down out of the corner of his eye. He had watched them together; he had seen the great love the man had for his little girl. That's why he had taken the food to them. But this was asking too much of him; he mustn't get involved. But, what if the man was really dying---and he could help him.

"Okay, kid, I'll see what I can do," he said reluctantly.

"Thank you, mister," she said, and taking hold of his hand she started back toward the beach. "If you're not God, who are you?"

"Why do you think I'm God?"

"Because you're not a raven, and only God or a raven could bring us food," she said, remembering the stories her daddy had told her from the Bible.

He remembered the stories from his childhood. "Well, I brought you the food, but I'm not God. My name is Jake."

"Are you a giant?"

"No, I'm just big," he answered.

"Big Jake," she mused. "I'll call you Big Jake."

"How did you get on the island?" he asked.

"I fell in the water and Daddy jumped in after me. We got carried a long ways from the boat by the waters; we were holding on to a log and Daddy let go and we went under the water, and God reached His big hands down and pulled us up out of the water and brought us here."

"You've sure got a big imagination," he told her.

"No, that's what really happened," she said firmly. "Daddy said so, and he knows, 'cause he's a preacher..."

"Preacher," Big Jake groaned, "that's all I need."

"Don't you like preachers, Big Jake?"

"I could live without them," he muttered as they reached the place where Brad was laying. He felt of his forehead. "High fever," he mumbled to himself. "I need a wet cloth."

Isabelle grabbed her jacket and dipped it into the water. She handed it to Big Jake, and for the first time she got a look at his face. "Your face is hurt," she cried. "How did your face get hurt?"

He pretended not to hear. "Come on," he said, "we're going to my place." He had some medicine there to help get the fever down and hopefully get the infection under control. "Leave everything here," he said, when she tried to get all their stuff together. He put Brad over his shoulder. They walked for a while, then, he stopped.

A makeshift cabin was hidden behind a clump of thick foliage. "Did you build this yourself," she asked as they went inside the cabin.

"Do you see anyone else around?" he snapped grumpily. "Didn't your mama teach you not to ask so many questions?" He laid Brad down on the bed.

Isabelle started crying. "I want my mommy," she sobbed, thinking about Roseanna.

"Kid, I'm sorry," he said, "that was thoughtless of me, but I don't have time to waste answering questions. I've got to try to help your daddy."

"I won't bother you anymore," she said sweetly. "Just make my daddy well." She started outside.

"Don't wander off," he cautioned. "The big bad wolf might get you."

She scurried back to his side.

He laughed. It was a nice laugh. Isabelle felt better just hearing it.

For the next couple of days, Brad teetered between life and death. One minute he was burning up with fever, the next he was shivering with chills. Big Jake kept wet towels on him for the fever, and covered him when the chills came. He got medicine down him as best he could. "Don't you die on me," he said, "there's no way I can take care of that kid."

Brad's fever broke on the third day. He opened his eyes. "Isabelle," he whispered, trying to get up.

"Don't try to get up," Big Jake said, holding him down on the bed, and giving him a drink of water.

"What have you done with Isabelle," Brad demanded feebly, trying again to get up.

Big Jake held him down. "Your little girl's all right," he assured him. "She's right here."

"Daddy!" Isabelle squealed happily. "You're awake." She ran to him and threw her arms around him. "I was so scared."

"What happened?" he asked, still dazed from the fever.

"You were sick, Daddy, and Big Jake brought you here, and he made you well."

"Thank you," Brad mumbled feebly. He tried to extend his hand to the man who had saved his life, but he was too weak.

"Don't mention it," Big Jake replied, keeping his head turned so Brad wouldn't see his face. "You need a lot of rest, and a lot of food, I suspect. How long has it been since you've had a good meal?"

"A while," Brad muttered softly, not wanting Isabelle to overhear. "I need some answers," he added.

"We're going to get some broth into you and then I want you to rest," Big Jake said. "We'll talk when you're feeling better."

Over the next few days, with lots of rest and some good solid food, Brad gradually regained his strength. "I feel up to talking now," he said one night after Isabelle had gone to sleep.

"I guess you want to know about my face," Big Jake said awkwardly.

"Not unless you want to tell me," Brad replied softly. "Is that the reason you're here on this island?

"Yeah," he said. "I couldn't cut it out in the real world after..." He stopped short.

"Jake, listen to me," Brad said, tenderly, "I know something terrible must have happened to you. It does help to talk about it, and I'm here to listen when you're ready."

"I used to be a teacher, and a pretty good one," Jake said, "before my world crashed down around me..." his voice trailed off as sadness overwhelmed him.

"What happened?" Brad's voice was gentle and filled with genuine concern.

"I had been out celebrating with friends, I'd had too much to drink, and like a fool, I got in my car and started home. I never made it. I ran into a bridge. I wasn't wearing my seat belt and my head crashed through the windshield. Can you believe that I came out of the wreck with just facial injuries? Some folks said I was lucky, that I could have died in the accident; well, they don't know how many times I've wished I had died that night."

"Don't say that, Jake," Brad said, compassionately. "God has a purpose for your life and..."

"Don't talk to me about God," he lashed out angrily.

"Surely, you can't blame God for your accident," Brad said, surprised that he would be angry with God for something that had been his fault.

"Not for the accident, I take full responsibility for that, but where was God after it happened, when I needed Him; when my heart cried out for help, where was He then?"

Brad was a little taken back by the question. He searched his mind for an answer. "I've never known God not to be there when someone cried out to Him for help," he stated truthfully. "Do you mind sharing with me why you believe God wasn't there for you?"

"After the accident, I tried to get on with my life," he said. "I returned to school, but the kids either made fun of me and called me 'monster face' or they were terrified of me and ran away. The school contacted me and said they were putting me on a leave of absence for the remainder of the school year, and could not renew my contract for the following year. I was still the same man, the same teacher, but because of the way I looked, I was no longer acceptable."

"Jake, it seems to me that you're blaming God for the actions of a few rude people. It's unfortunate; but there are people like that in world. But if you'll take the time to look, you will find that there are so many more folks who wouldn't care about the scars on your face, they would accept you just the way you are."

"What planet are you from?" he asked sarcastically. "On planet earth, there's no place for a man with a disfigured face." His voice broke. "And don't tell me that God will make things better; my mother is a praying woman and she prayed many prayers in my behalf; I even tried praying some myself, but did things get better; no the jeers and taunts got worse; until finally I decided to end it all."

"What made you change your mind?"

"This may sound silly, but I met this girl; it's not what you think; I went to this concert to hear Roseanna sing..."

"Roseanna!" Brad exclaimed, excitement in his voice. "You know Roseanna!"

"Yeah, she's this country singer," he explained. "I guess you know her, too, huh?"

Brad smiled. "I'm married to her."

"Roseanna is your wife; the kid's mother?"

Brad nodded. "How did meeting Roseanna change your mind?" he asked eagerly.

"Roseanna was my favorite singer of all times," he said. "When I heard she was coming to town, I wanted to see her in person and hear her sing one more time, so I went to the concert. For some reason she had come down into the audience before the concert, and as she started to go backstage, she saw me and stopped; she shook hands with me and looked at me as if I were a normal person; like she didn't even notice the scars, she noticed me. She talked to me a minute, then smiled that famous smile of hers and promised to sing a song just for me. The song she dedicated to me was "Dreams"; and I left the concert feeling like my dreams really could come true; what she did for me that night kept me from taking my life."

"That sounds like my Roseanna," Brad said beaming. "She spreads sunshine every where she goes."

"But then I had to go back out into the real world and I realized that nothing had changed; so I got the money I'd saved over the years and bought all the supplies I could, I loaded them aboard my boat and sailed off to find a secluded island where I would never have to come face to face with another living soul 'til the day I died. And it was working 'til you two showed up."

"You have a boat?" Brad asked excitedly.

"We're sitting in it," he said. "I used it to help build this cabin."

Brad sighed dejectedly. "Do you know where we are?"

"I don't know exactly where we are," Jake answered. "I do know we're on one of the islands in the Bahamas."

"The Bahamas. It shouldn't be too hard to find us." Brad's voice had a ring of excitement to it. "We're not too far away from Florida..."

"Don't get your hopes up," Jake said. "There's seven hundred islands in the Bahamas and only about forty of them are occupied. It's not likely that anyone will ever find us here."

"We've got to figure out a way to get off this island," Brad said. "We've got to get back home, back to Roseanna."

"I can imagine what she's going through thinking you and the kid are dead." He hesitated a moment. "I'll do anything I can to help."

"There is something you can to help right now," Brad said thoughtfully. "I don't want Isabelle to fall behind in her studies, so I've been trying to teach her, but my skills as a teacher are sadly limited, so if you would agree to teach her..."

"I'll be happy too," Jake said, with a spark in his eyes. "It will feel good to be teaching again."

"Our teaching supplies are limited," Brad explained, " a sharp stick, and the sand."

"I think we can do better than that," Jake told him. "I have all kinds of books, as well as paper and pencils, paints, and also some games."

"Praise the Lord!" Brad exclaimed happily. "That's another prayer He has answered for me."

Chapter 19

"I didn't know you were Roseanna's little girl," Big Jake told Isabelle the next morning.

"You know my mommy!" she exclaimed.

"Yeah, I met her once at a concert," he said. "She's terrific. You look a lot like her, you know."

Isabelle beamed. Then a sad look crossed her face. "I miss my mommy and I want to see her."

"We're going to do everything we can to get you home to her," he said, "but until we do, I've got a surprise for you."

"What?" Isabelle asked eagerly. She loved surprises and it had been a while since she'd had a pleasant one.

"We're going to have real school," he said, "with a real schoolteacher, real books, and pencils and paper." He handed her a book.

Her eyes twinkled as she leafed through it, looking at the brightly colored pictures. "Thank you, Big Jake," she exclaimed happily. "Are you a real schoolteacher?"

"I used to be," he said, "but don't thank me just yet. We're going to work hard at this. We're going to do reading, spelling, writing, arithmetic and art each day until we're about ready to drop in our tracks."

"Let's get started," she said excitedly.

They spent all morning on the schoolwork. She learned several new words and how to spell a couple of them. They did simple addition, and she practiced writing her ABC's. "We'll do art after lunch," he told her.

Brad had lunch waiting for them. The vegetable soup and crackers tasted so good.

"I wish I knew what day it is," Brad said, with a faraway look in his eyes. "Mine and Roseanna's anniversary is May 1, and I'm sure it's getting close to that date."

Jake walked over and moved some books off a shelf he had made. "There's a calendar underneath all this junk," he said. "I can tell you in a minute."

"After all these years, how do you keep count of the days?" Brad asked puzzled.

"After the first year, I merely started over, writing each new date on the day it came on, and I've done that for over seven years now."

"You've been here that long?" Isabelle exclaimed. She couldn't really comprehend how long seven years was, but it must be a long time, cause she was almost six years old, and that was a very long time.

"Today is May 1," Jake commented, ignoring Isabelle's question, and showing Brad the calendar. He saw the look on Brad's face and sensed he needed to be alone. "Eat up, kid," he said. "We'll go down to the beach and see what we can find to paint."

"I'm almost ready," she said, digging into her food with a passion.

"I'm going to find a quiet spot and be alone with my thoughts," Brad said, as they got ready to leave. He needed some time alone with Roseanna, on this, their special day. He needed to tell her how much he loved her. He needed to reach out to her with his love. He walked around the island 'til he found a spot that reminded him a little of Roseanna's special place back home. He sat down on a log, leaned his head against a tree, and let all the love he felt for her flow through him. He thought back to their wedding day and how he had been the happiest man in the world when he saw his beautiful Roseanna walking up the aisle to him. He thought he could never love her more than he did at that moment; but now seven years later, his love for her had grown even more. "My darling," he said, "I hope where ever you are right now, you can feel my love for you. I know you're thinking of me; of this day; and of the life we've shared together. I know you're heartbroken, thinking that you've lost me forever; cause I know how I would feel if I lost you, my sweet Roseanna. Sweetheart, I'm sending all the love in my heart out to you. I hope you can feel it, and know that I am thinking of you today; that even if I were gone, I would still have you in my heart, and that our love will truly last throughout all of eternity. I will come back to you, I promise. Hold on, sweetheart, a while longer and Isabelle and I will be back in your arms where we belong." Tears flowed down his face as he longed to see her, hold her in his arms and kiss her. "Oh, my darling, what you must be going through." He prayed for her from the depths of his heart. "Father, help her. Bring some sunshine into her life until we can get back to her. Don't let her suffer alone." He spent the rest of the afternoon thinking about her.

Isabelle and Big Jake sat on the beach painting. She painted green water at the bottom of the sheet of drawing paper. "You draw good," she said, looking at his painting, "but there's no boat out there."

"I know," he said, adding the final touches to the sails on the boat. "I paint what I see up here," he said, pointing to his head, "and I see a boat out there."

She quickly painted a sailboat on her picture. "I see a boat too," she said, "and I see Mommy in the boat and she's coming to get us." She drew a picture of a lady with long brown hair, standing in the boat.

"You really miss your mother, don't you?" he asked, seeing the pain in her eyes.

She nodded, as a tear rolled down her face. "Do you have a mommy, Big Jake? Do you miss her?"

He fought back the tears that were welling up in his eyes. This kid could really get to him. "Yeah, I have a mother and I do miss her," he said, with a faraway look in his eyes.

"Did you get in a storm and get lost from her, too?"

"No, I came here because I wanted to."

"You wanted to get lost from your mommy?" Isabelle cried, not able to believe that he would choose to be away from his mother.

"Well," he stammered, "it wasn't my mother I wanted to get away from, it was all those other people."

"Big Jake, why did you run away from those other people?"

"Kid, you ask too many questions," he said, not wanting to talk about his reasons for leaving.

"Is your mommy sad," she asked, ignoring his last comment.

"I'm sure she's sad," he replied, feeling a pang of guilt tear at his insides.

"My mommy's sad, too," she said. "I pray for her everyday. Do you pray for your mommy, Big Jake?"

He shook his head. "I don't pray, period," he informed her, a bit tartly.

"You don't want God to help you?" she asked in surprise, then pausing a moment she added, "I'm going to pray for your mommy; and for you."

"That's fine, kid," he said, a twinge in his voice. "Now, let's get back to the cabin; lessons are over for today."

She took his hand, and holding on tightly she skipped back across the island, keeping pace with his big steps.

"We've got to find some clothes for you two," Jake said that night as Brad sat braiding Isabelle's long brown hair into one loose braid. "Brad, you can wear some of my

139

things; they'll be big but they will do; but, what about the kid?"

"She can wear my shirt," Brad said, pointing to the blue pullover shirt he had on. "I'll tear the sleeves out and it will be okay."

"Hold on," Jake said, pulling out a big box. "When I was getting ready to leave, I got some material from my mother's sewing box, as well as a pair of scissors. I thought they might come in handy; let's see what we can find."

They found several pieces of material, in bright colors of pink, yellow, blue and red. They set out to fashion dresses for Isabelle to wear. They cut each piece of cloth into appropriate lengths for her, cut a slit in the middle for her head to go through, and then cut a long sash for each outfit, to tie around her waist.

"You'll be dressed just like the natives," Big Jake laughingly told her.

Isabelle squealed with delight, trying on each new outfit. "They're pretty," she said, hugging Brad and Big Jake.

Later, after Brad put Isabelle to bed, he turned to Big Jake. "We need to come up with plans on how to get off this island. Maybe some way to get a ship to notice us."

Big Jake shook his head. "In all the years I've been here, I've never seen a ship close enough to the island to be able to see anyone or anything that's here..."

"Maybe, if we build a big fire, that would get their attention," Brad suggested.

"We could set the entire island on fire and no one would notice," Jake said. "The only ships I've ever seen are just specks on the horizon. They never come anywhere close to here. We're going to have to find another way."

"Any suggestions?"

Jake shook his head again. "We'll have to find a way to build a raft, but that's not going to be easy, we need the right kind of lumber or logs."

Brad looked around the cabin. "These planks were off your boat, right?"

"Don't even go there," Jake said.

"But we could use them as a means to get off the island..."

"And, what am I supposed to do?" Jake asked a bit angrily.

"You'll go with us, of course," Brad replied.

"No, I won't," he declared bluntly. "I'm staying right here."

"We can't go and leave you here," Brad told him. "Your supplies won't last forever. When they run out what will you do?"

"I'll deal with that when it happens," he snapped. "I'd rather take my chances here than to go back and face the world I left behind."

Brad felt an overwhelming compassion for the man sitting here before him. "Jake," he said, "if your scars bother you so much, there are ways to conceal them. Why don't you grow a beard? They're quite fashionable."

"After the accident, I tried that, but something happened when they did surgery on my face, and, now, I can't grow a beard at all."

"What about cosmetic surgery?" Brad asked. "They can do wonders today..."

"Yes, if you're rich," he answered quickly. "I couldn't afford it then, and I certainly can't afford it now."

"That's no problem," Brad told him. "Roseanna has more money than all of us could ever spend, and more coming in each day; she'd be happy to pay all of your medical bills."

"I couldn't let her do that," he protested. "She doesn't owe me anything."

"You saved our lives, Jake," Brad said gently. "She'd gladly give all of her money, everything she owns to get us back. Besides, she doesn't need a reason; she helps people because she wants to, not because she owes them. Please, come back with us and let us help you."

"What if the surgery didn't work, I'd be in the same boat as I was before. No, thanks, I'll stay right here," Jake said determinedly.

A frown crossed Brad's face. He couldn't leave Jake here, but how could he persuade him to come with them, when they found a way to get off the island? Jake needed the Lord; then he would find the hope and courage he needed to face the world again. That was the answer, help Jake find the Lord and the Lord would do the rest. "Father, was Isabelle and I put here on this island for such a time as this?" he pondered silently in his heart. "Give me the wisdom, Lord, to know how to do Your will."

Big Jake's thoughts were troubled as he mulled the situation over in his mind. He couldn't let these people get to him. He had settled down on the island and he was content here; now they were threatening to disrupt his whole way of life. He could brush Brad off; but the kid, she got to him; that sweet smile and those never ending questions---he had to find a way to get them out of here.

Brad broke the silence. "Isabelle's birthday is the middle of June," he commented, "what a wonderful birthday present that would be; to reunite her with her mother and the rest of the family."

"We'll see what we can do," Jake replied, wanting to get Isabelle and Brad back home for their sakes, as well as his.

Isabelle's birthday came and they were no closer to finding a way off the island than before.

"Daddy," she said wistfully, "does Mommy know it's my birthday?"

"Of course she knows, sweetheart," Brad answered tearfully, holding her in his arms. This was so hard on her. And what it must be doing to Roseanna. She always went all out for Isabelle's birthday parties. Last year she had rented ponies for each child at the party, and horses for the adults; they took hot dogs, chips, and birthday cake, rode to the lake and had a wiener roast. What a good time they'd had. A tear rolled down his face as he thought of Roseanna alone this year with no Isabelle to hold, no party to plan. "God, please help her," he prayed.

"Daddy, Mommy's very sad, today. I wish we could be there to make her happy again," Isabelle said wistfully.

"I wish that, too, my precious girl."

"Isabelle, we don't have a cake for your birthday, but we can light a candle and you can blow it out, and make a wish," Big Jake said later. He lit the candle. He and Brad sang their version of "Happy Birthday" to Isabelle.

"I wish with all of my heart that my mommy won't be sad anymore," Isabelle said, blowing out the candle.

Brad's heart swelled with pride for his daughter; she could have wished for something for herself; instead, she was thinking of Roseanna, and wanted her to be happy. "Thank You, God for such a wonderful little girl, and make her wish come true; send some happiness into Roseanna's life," he prayed as a tear rolled down his face, "and, Father, help us get back home to her."

Big Jake squeezed back the tears that were trying to come into his eyes. He had never seen a kid like her. He had to find a way to make her wish come true; he had to get her back home to her mother. Only then would all of them be happy.

Chapter 20

Months past. Summer turned to fall, at least on the calendar. You could hardly tell one season from another as the temperature changed very little from summer to winter. They had not come up with a way to get off the island.

Jake had brought seeds with him, but the soil on the island was not very good for raising vegetables, so they only got a small amount of produce for their efforts; but the tomatoes, cucumbers, cabbage, peppers, onions, beans, peas, potatoes, okra and corn that did survive tasted so good. They found many different ways to eat each one separately, as well as put it all together to make a stew.

They had also done a lot of fishing and hunting to supplement their food supply; marsh hens, quail, ducks and wild hogs were a part of the daily menu. "We can kill the wild boars now that there's three of us to eat the meat," Jake said. "I never tried before because there would have been so much waste."

"The shot we heard that night," Brad said, reflecting back, "that was you hunting. You don't know how much you scared us."

"Back then, I didn't care if I scared you," Big Jake stated. "I didn't want you on the island in the first place."

"If you resented us so much, why did you bring us those supplies," Brad quizzed. "Why didn't you just leave us to our own devices?"

"You wouldn't have lasted two weeks here without help," Jake said. "I didn't want you on the island, but I couldn't let you die."

"We owe our lives to you, Jake," Brad said, "I hope someday we can find a way to repay you. What can you give a man who has given your life back to you?"

"Just find a way to get the kid back to her mother," Jake replied somberly. He had grown to love Isabelle deeply, and the thought of her being separated from the mother she loved and needed, was more than he could bear. His number one priority was to get her back home, but how? He wasn't ready to dismantle his cabin in order to build a raft. What if it didn't work? They would be worse off then now. No, they'd have to find another way.

Isabelle spoke up. "Daddy, will we ever get to go home? Will we ever see Mommy again," she asked, her lips trembling.

Brad could see she was losing hope, and he must not let that happen. "Sure, we will, baby," he replied, giving her a big hug. "It's just taking longer than we thought."

"What if Mommy forgets us, what if she stops loving us?" The tears were flowing down her face now as she voiced her fears aloud.

"Oh, my darling girl, Mommy could never forget us, and she could never stop loving us either." He pulled her into his arms and held on to her as sobs racked her body.

"Is Mommy still married to us, Daddy?"

"Yes, sweetheart, Mommy is still married to us," he assured her. "Why do you ask, Isabelle?"

"I dreamed that Mommy was in a dark place, and we were there, but she didn't know us anymore, and she didn't love us."

"Don't cry, baby, it was just a bad dream. Everything will be okay. I promise. Mommy will always love us."

She finally calmed down and wiped her tears. "Daddy, I'm glad that Mommy loves us," she said, giving him a hug, "and that Big Jake is going to get us home."

Her childlike faith had been restored by a few words from the father that she loved and trusted.

Brad was glad that he had soothed Isabelle's fears but she had brought up a haunting question. It had been over five months since the accident. What if they didn't get home for years, or never? Roseanna thought they were dead; would she move on with her life? Would she find a new love? Brad winced as he thought of her in someone else's arms. Could she love another man as she loved him? *'Til death do us part, 'til death do us part.* The words rang in his ears. She would believe that she was free to love again, to marry again. But *their* love would last for all of eternity, they both had said so; still, she was a young woman, and she faced years of loneliness ahead of her. Would he want her to go through life alone, or would he want her to find happiness with another man? Part of him, the selfish part, wanted her to be his, and his alone, forever. But the part of him that loved her more than life itself, wanted her to be happy, to find love again with a good man, and raise a family. He didn't want her to go through life, hanging on to memories and dreams that could never be fulfilled.

His thoughts were troubled. He walked away from the cabin and found a place where he could talk to God alone.

"Oh, Father, if we're never going to get off this island, if I'm never going to be a husband to Roseanna again, please release her from the vows we made. I know only death can actually release her, but to her I am dead; so Lord, don't hold her to those vows. And, please, Father, set her heart free to love someone else the way she loves me."

Brad's faith had never wavered as much as it did now, as he looked ahead to the future, a bleak future for Isabelle and him. The situation seemed hopeless. They were not going to get off the island. And what about when their food ran out? How long could they survive? His heart

146

cried out as he thought of Isabelle spending the rest of her life, marooned here on this island, never to live as she should, never to know the pleasures of growing up in a normal world; never to feel the joy of being in her mothers arms again. He wept before the Lord as these pictures of the future rumbled through his mind.

From the depths of his tortured soul, words from his favorite Bible passage, Psalms 91, came to him. He quoted them, in his own words, as a heartfelt prayer.

"He that dwelleth in the secret place of the most High shall abide under the shadow of the Almighty...I will say of the Lord, He is my refuge and my fortress: my God; in him will I trust...He shall cover me with his feathers and under his wings will I trust: his truth shall be my shield and buckler...I shall not be afraid for the terror by night; nor for the arrow that flies by day; nor for the pestilence that walks in the darkness...He has given his angels charge over me, to keep me safe...I will call upon him and He will answer me: He will be with me in trouble; He will deliver me..."

Tears rolled down his face. "Thank you, God for reminding me of who You are, and that You love me and will always be here when I need You; and forgive me for doubting." He got up with a renewed spirit within him: he knew that it was done: in God's time they *were* going home.

Chapter 21

Brad never lost the assurance that he received that day in prayer. He didn't know when, he didn't know how; but he knew they were going home. All the efforts, he and Jake had made to build a raft had failed. Brad knew there was some reason they were still on the island, and he had a pretty good notion what it was. It was because of Jake. He needed to find the Lord; and maybe Brad and Isabelle were the ones to lead him. "Father, use us to help him find peace," Brad prayed as compassion for Big Jake swept over him. No longer was he thinking of himself and Isabelle getting off the island, but of the man he had come to care about, the man who had saved them, the man who had known so much sorrow in his life. "Lord, show me the way to reach him."

The answer hit him like a thunderbolt. It was so simple. He couldn't believe he hadn't thought of it before, especially with him being a preacher. The next day was Sunday so he could get started on his plan right away. "We're having church tomorrow," he announced that night at supper. He borrowed paper and pencil from Jake and wrote scriptures from memory as he prepared his sermon for tomorrow's service. He prayed earnestly for God's direction.

Sunday morning dawned bright and clear. Brad was excited. It felt good to be preaching again, even to such a small congregation. He could hardly wait to see how Jake would react to the service. Would he be saved the first day? Would he allow Christ to speak peace to his heart? And, if he did, would that change his mind about going home? He could only pray that it would.

Brad had set up a pulpit under a tree close to the cabin. Isabelle was there early, sitting in a folding chair that Jake brought with him when he came to the island. She was excited about having church.

"Are we going to have Sunday School, too, Daddy?" she asked.

"Not today, sweetie, maybe we'll work up lessons for next week," he told her, remembering how much she loved Sunday School. "I wonder where Jake is?" he asked, anxious to get started.

"He took his fishing pole and went towards the beach," Isabelle replied. "Said he was going to catch our supper."

Brad let out a sigh of disappointment. Jake wouldn't be here. Should he forget the service? "No, I'll go ahead with it, just as if he were here," Brad said under his breath. "Lord, I'll do my part, the rest is up to you."

"Daddy, I want to sing," Isabelle said when Brad finished his sermon. He nodded and she walked to the pulpit and stood beside him. She started singing.

"Jesus loves me, this I know,
For the Bible tells me so;
Little ones to Him belong,
They are weak, but He is strong.
Yes, Jesus loves me, Yes Jesus loves me,
Yes, Jesus loves me, the Bible tells me so."

Brad wiped a tear away as he listened to her sing. She sounded so much like Roseanna. "You sing like an angel," he told her when she finished the song. He ended the service with prayer.

Big Jake wiped a tear away as he listened to Isabelle sing. That song took him back to one day when he was a child, sitting in Sunday School. The teacher led them in singing that very song. He had felt a warm glow in his heart. When the song ended he raised his hand. "Teacher, I know God loves the whole world, but does He really love *me*?"

The teacher walked over and put her arm around him. "Yes, Jake, He really loves you. He died on the cross for you..."

"He did that for me?" Jake blurted out; and he remembered thinking how neat it was that someone would do that for him. That day he had given his heart to the Lord.

He fought the tears that were filling his eyes. He had to get his mind on other things. He wasn't ready to deal with these feelings yet. What had drawn him back to the cabin so soon? He had meant to fish until they were finished with the church service.

Isabelle caught sight of him and ran over to him. "Big Jake," she exclaimed, "you missed the church service. Daddy preached real good and I sang."

"I bet you sang good, too," he replied, wiping the last tear from his eye.

"I wish you had been here," she said, all bubbly. "Why did you go fishing and miss church, Big Jake?"

"Church is not my cup of tea..."

"You don't like church!" she blurted out. "Why don't you like church?"

"You ask too many questions, kid," he said. "Now, let's go eat lunch, then we'll clean the fish I caught this morning, and I'll fix them on the grill, the way you like them, and, just maybe we can find some potatoes to go with them."

"Thank you," she said excitedly. "I love you, Big Jake. Do you love me?"

"Yeah, I love you, kid," he muttered, as if it didn't matter; but he knew it mattered. He had purposed in his heart never to get close to another human being as long as he lived, and he had succeeded until she came along. He couldn't deny that he loved her; that she was important to him, and that she had brought sunshine into his life, a life he thought would never see sunshine again.

Things went on as usual for the next couple of weeks. Brad had church on Sundays and Jake found excuses not to be there. He wasn't ready yet to listen to anything that God's word had to say. He didn't believe anymore that God loved him; maybe God loved the world as a whole, but He sure didn't care about people. If He did, how could He let Isabelle be torn out of the arms of her mother; a mother she loved and adored, and needed so much. How could He keep them separated? And what about Brad? He had preached the gospel all these years, and how had God repaid him; by tearing him apart from his wife, the one person he loved more than anyone else in the world; and Roseanna, the agony she must be going through; none of them deserved this. Could a God who loved them do this to them? Maybe he deserved what he got, because of his careless actions the night of the accident, but these people had done nothing to deserve all this pain they were going through. They'd been on this island six months now, and were no closer to getting off then when they first came. If God loved them, why did He let them suffer this way? Brad and Isabelle seemed to take comfort in believing that God loved them; and that was okay for them; but not for him. He was glad he hadn't given into those feelings that had been coming over him lately, the urge to give God another chance.

"Jake, you've done wonders with Isabelle," Brad remarked, interrupting his thoughts. "With all the things you've taught her, she will be way ahead of her class when we get home." He said it as if it were a fact, and not just wishful thinking on his part. "She missed the last couple of months of kindergarten and the first couple of months of first grade, but thanks to you she hasn't fallen behind in her studies."

"Happy I could help," Jake said, a certain pride in his voice for a job well done. He was still a good teacher and that made him feel good. "Speaking of school, it's time for art class, Isabelle."

They grabbed their art supplies and headed for the beach. Brad went along. He would sit close by and write scriptures and study for Sunday's sermon. One day Jake would run out of excuses for not attending church, and Brad wanted to be ready when that day came.

"You paint good," Isabelle told Big Jake, later, as they sat painting. "But why are your pictures so sad?"

"What do you think my pictures are sad?" he asked.

"You're skies are always dark, no happy clouds or sunshine," she said. "Are you sad, Big Jake?"

"Yeah, I suppose I'm sad," he answered.

"Why are you sad?"

"Kid, take a good look at me," he said, hoping an honest answer would stop all her questions. "See how ugly I am..."

"You're not ugly, Big Jake," she piped up. "Your face is just hurt. It can get fixed, and then you won't have to be sad anymore. I don't want you to be sad. I love you." She walked over to him and kissed him on the cheek.

"I love you, too, kid." There, he had said the words out loud, he had admitted it, without any prompting on her part this time.

She sat down to paint again but stopped when she noticed something in the water. "Daddy. Big Jake," she yelled excitedly. "There's something in the water, something pink, and it's coming here." She ran into the water.

"Isabelle, be careful," Brad warned, running into the water after her.

"It's a pink flower," she exclaimed happily. "Look! There's more pink flowers. I love pink, do you think God sent these pink flowers to me, Daddy?"

Brad picked up one of the roses. "I don't know, sweetheart," he said, then he gasped as he saw more flowers floating toward them. "Yellow roses," he whispered, and reached down and lifted them out of the water. Tears were streaming down his face. "Roseanna, my darling," he cried, remembering the yellow roses that adorned the church the day of their wedding. The sweet memories of that day overwhelmed him as a desire to see his precious Roseanna and hold her in his arms consumed him. "Isabelle, these flowers are a message from Mommy; a message that says she still loves us and she is thinking of us."

"Did Mommy put the flowers in the water, Daddy?" Did she send them to us?"

"I don't know who put the flowers in the water, baby, but I do know they are a sign from God to let us know that Mommy is thinking about us."

"I want to keep my flowers forever," Isabelle said, caressing the petals of the roses.

"Sweetheart, they won't last much longer," Brad told her, trying to get control of his emotions.

"We'll press them in a book," Big Jake said, "that way you can keep them forever."

Isabelle smiled, then, a worried look crossed her face. "When we leave the island, will you remember to get the flowers out of your book and give them to me? I want to show them to Mommy."

"I'll give you the whole book," he said, a catch in his voice. She was so sure that she was going home.

"Let's go and do it right now," she said excitedly. "Daddy, do you want to put your flowers in a book, too?"

"Maybe later," he said. "I'm going to stay here a while longer." He wanted to be alone with his thoughts, to sort them out. He had blurted out to Isabelle about this being a sign, but was it really, or was it just a coincidence, a freak of nature that sent the flowers to the island where they were. Pink and yellow roses; pink was Isabelle's favorite color; yellow was the color of the roses at their wedding. What were the chances of that just happening---one in a million? It was almost as if he could feel and smell Roseanna's touch on the roses as he held them close to him. He didn't know how the flowers got in the water; or who put them there, but he could feel her presence when he touched them; so he knew they were a sign from God to let him know that Roseanna was still thinking of them, and that they would be going home soon. "Hold on a little while longer, sweetheart, we're coming home to you."

Chapter 22

"Belle, they're gone. My Brad and Isabelle are gone forever," Roseanna cried, standing in the little white church, clinging to her sister, a couple of days after going to the ocean to say goodbye to them. "How am I going to go through the rest of my life without Brad and Isabelle, when I can't even face one tomorrow without them?"

Belle held her close and cried along with her. "Oh, Sis, I wish I could take the pain away."

"I know they're gone; but in my heart they're still alive," she said, between sobs. "I've got to let them go, but it's so hard. I love them so much."

"I know," Belle whispered, stroking her hair. Belle's heart ached; Roseanna was hurting and there was no way she could help her; nothing she could do to fill the emptiness in her sister's heart. "Roseanna, put this in God's Hands; let Him help you," she prompted.

"God has helped me a lot," Roseanna told her. "I couldn't have made it this far without Him. But the grief and pain is still there. I think it always will be."

Belle nodded. She knew how strong Roseanna's love was for Brad and Isabelle. She knew her sister would never get over losing them. But she also knew that Roseanna had to go on; she couldn't live in the past; she had to look to the future. "The baby will make it a little easier," she said, "just think about your son and the good times you two will share together.

"You're right, I've got to stop this," Roseanna said, trying to dry her tears. "It can't be good for my baby. He needs to feel loved, but I don't have time for him when my heart is consumed with hurt and grief. Belle, please help me."

"You know I will, hon, just tell me what to do."

Roseanna shook her head. "I don't know," she cried, "I don't know what to do."

"What about Andy?" Belle asked. "You seem happy when he's around."

"Andy is wonderful, but he wants me to marry him and I just can't, Belle. I don't love him in that way. I could never be a wife to him as long as my heart is filled with love for Brad."

"Didn't you tell me that Andy knows how you feel and he still wants to marry you?"

Roseanna nodded her head. " But I can't let him make that sacrifice," she said. "I love him too much to let him settle for second best. I can't do that to Andy."

"Can't do what to me?" Andy asked walking in on the conversation.

"Remember, you do love him," Belle leaned over and whispered in her sister's ear. Aloud she said, "I need to be going. I've got to fix supper. Andy, will you walk me to my car?"

"Belle, what do you want to tell me that you didn't want Roseanna to hear?" he asked once they were outside.

"Was I that obvious?" she asked, then, continued. "I'm worried about my sister. I know that you've asked her to marry you, and I know the reasons why she won't. They are pretty valid reasons; but I hope you don't give up on her, 'cause I believe you're her only chance at happiness."

Andy grinned. "The words 'give up' are not in my vocabulary," he assured her. "I have no intentions of giving up on her and the life we can have together." He opened the door for Belle and helped her in the car. "Goodbye, little sister," he said, winking at her.

Belle smiled and drove away. She liked him. He was good for Roseanna; just what she needed in her life now. She only hoped her sister would realize that.

"What is it that you can't do to me?" Andy asked again, walking over to the parsonage with Roseanna.

"I can't marry you."

He took her hand. "Roseanna, I've heard all your arguments, and I don't agree; I believe you can marry me..."

"But I'm in love with Brad," she interrupted, "I thought when I went to the ocean and said goodbye to them, it would be easier, but in my heart he is still alive, and he always will be; how can I marry you when I feel like I'm still married to him; when I'm still grieving for him?"

He weighed his words carefully. "The pain will get more bearable, I promise; not today, nor tomorrow, maybe not next month, but someday things will get better. You'll be able to walk out of this tempest of grief and pain, and into the sunshine beyond it."

"Have you been able to do that?" she asked, tearfully. "Is the pain you feel over losing Emily getting easier to bear?"

"I will always grieve over the loss of Emily, and what might have been if she had not died, and I will always love her; but, yes, I am beginning to walk towards the sunshine; and it's mostly because of you. Maybe, we can never have with each other, what we had with Emily and Brad, but that doesn't mean we can't have a good life together." He put his arms around her. "Let's do this together, Roseanna. Let me help you through this tempest, let me help you get to the other side."

"You don't know how much I wish I could say yes," she sobbed. "I want you in my life, Andy, but it wouldn't be fair to you to be tied to a wife who could never love you the way you deserved to be loved. Keep walking toward the

157

sunlight, Andy, I can't ask you to stay here in the shadows with me..."

"Roseanna, I could never be in the shadows as long as I'm with you," he said. "You are the sunshine in my life. Without you, I would be in the shadows."

"But someday, you might find someone you could love, in the way a man should love the woman he marries," she argued. "I can't chance standing in the way of your happiness.

"Roseanna, you are my happiness," he said. "My commitment to you will be forever. I will dedicate the rest of my life to making you and little Will happy; and that will make me happy."

He was more like Brad then any man she'd ever known, so loving and giving. She leaned over and kissed him, casually. "I do love you, Andy, but I can't give you the answer you want to hear; not yet. I need some time to think and to pray about this. I need God's guidance."

"We both need that," he said, "so I won't push you for an answer. Just let me know. In the meantime, I'll pray too." He could see she needed time to settle the issue in her mind and her heart. She needed time to heal.

"Thank's, Andy. I promise I won't keep you waiting long."

"You said you bought some land to build a new house," he stated, changing the subject. "How's that coming along?"

She sighed. "Brad and I bought that land together, to build our dream house one day. I don't know if I can do it without him."

"Honey," he said, trying to find the right words, "maybe you need to go ahead with some of the plans you and Brad made; that way you can keep a part of him alive in your life, as well as in your heart. I wish I'd had some plans with Emily that I could hold on to, but we didn't have enough time together to make any real plans, we only had dreams, and they all died with her."

"I do need to get started on it," she said. "The church will be getting a new pastor and they will need the parsonage. Brad sketched out some rough plans. They're around here some where." She searched through his desk. "Here they are." She unrolled them and laid them on the desk. Her throat tightened. "Brad," she whispered, running her hand over the drawings and the words he had written there. She wiped the tears away.

"Is this too rough on you, Roseanna," Andy asked solemnly, not wanting to put more on her than she was able to bear. Even though Brad had been gone for months, Roseanna was just now, having to face the memories here in the home they had shared together. "We can do this another time."

"No, you're right," she said, "I do need to get started on this, and it wouldn't be any easier a year from now. Building this house the way Brad and I planned will be like having a part of him and Isabelle with me every day for the rest of my life. They will be a part of every room in the house. Thanks for suggesting this, Andy."

"I'll make some coffee and we'll get busy going over the plans," he said.

They mulled over the plans while drinking coffee and eating donuts. "This was Brad's office," Roseanna said, pointing to a room off the living room. "I told him a room at the back of the house would be quieter, but he wanted to be near Isabelle and me; said he could study better when we were close by. We included an outside entrance to his office so folks who needed counseling, or just wanted to talk to him, wouldn't have to come through the rest of the house. Here's the master bedroom with a double closet all the way across one wall, one for me and one for Brad. This was Isabelle's room, with a playroom separating it from another bedroom, in case we ever had another child. Now we're having a son, and Brad will never know him." Tears started down her face again.

"I think this is a mistake," Andy said, trying to console her. "We need to put this away for now."

"No, I've got to do this," she told him.

Andy felt admiration for this man who filled every inch of Roseanna's being. He could tell from the look of love in her eyes every time she spoke of him that he was one in a million. No one could ever compete with him for her heart.

"This is our dream kitchen," she said, "it's big and roomy with lots of cabinets and all kinds of built in gadgets."

"We can add a work island right here," Andy said, pointing to the middle of the kitchen, "that way it will be close to both the stove and the sink and will save us time and lots of steps when we're working in there."

"I like that idea," Roseanna said and smiled. He had used the word, 'we', so easy, without giving it any thought. Was he really that confident that he would be a part of her life from now on? Is that what she wanted? Being around him seemed natural, but did she want to marry him? Could she ever give up being Mrs. Bradley Lefourche? "I don't think so," she mumbled under her breath.

The next day Roseanna called a contractor and commissioned him to build the house, and to do it as quickly as possible without taking any shortcuts. She told him to use the best materials, and hire the most qualified men to do the job. The dreams they shared would be wrapped up in this house, so everything would be just the way she and Brad had planned it, except for the work island which Andy had suggested.

For the next month, Roseanna watched as the house took shape. At the rate they were going, she could move in by Christmas. Christmas in her own house; the house she was to have shared with Brad and Isabelle? Could she be happy there? She would like to stay where she was, amid all the memories of past days, when she was happy and her life was filled with love and laughter. Those memories were sweet to her now and she wanted to cling to them forever. But, Brother Troasclair would have to appoint a new pastor soon. When they moved in, they would make new memories there, and all the old ones would be pushed aside and forgotten, lost somewhere in the shadows of the place she used to call home. A tear ran down her face. "Oh, God, all those precious memories, don't let them be lost forever." she prayed. She would go through every nook and cranny of that house and commit each memory to her mind and to her journal. She wanted to remember every minute of their life together. There would be no memories of Brad and Isabelle in the new house, no special place where Brad had kissed her; no spot where Isabelle had sat her dolls around her little table for a tea party; none of their happy laughter ringing out through the rooms; so she had to store up all of the ones from the parsonage, and tuck them away in a special place in her heart, never to be forgotten.

She wept as she looked at the house under construction. "Brad," she cried, "our dream house, all the plans we made, the happy years we were going to spend together here, and now you and Isabelle will never share it with me and little Will. When I think that you will never know your son, or that he will never know you, my heart breaks inside me..." She spun her wheels as she sped away from the house, blinded by the tears flowing down her face. She had to find Andy. She had to talk to him.

Chapter 23

Roseanna pulled into the churchyard. Andy's car was parked there. She jumped out of the car and ran into the church. "Andy," she gasped.

He turned at the sound of her voice. "Roseanna..."

"Andy, I hate that house, make them tear it down," she sobbed, falling into his arms.

"I don't understand," he said, "what's wrong with the house?"

"It's our house; Brad's, Isabelle's and mine; but they won't ever live there, and I don't want to either. I don't ever want to see it again." She trembled in his arms.

"Honey, listen to me," Andy said gently, "you've got to get hold of yourself. This is not good for you or the baby. Don't worry about the house, I'll stop construction on it first thing tomorrow," he promised, feeling certain she would change her mind and want to finish it some day. "We're going to pray, Roseanna, for God to give you relief from this pain you feel, but you've got to want to let go of it. You've got to let them go..."

She wrenched free of his arms. "I'll never let them go!" she cried. "How could you even suggest such a thing?"

"Roseanna, this may seem cruel to you, but I'm saying it out of love and concern for you and your baby. What would Brad want you to do?" he asked bluntly. "Would he want you to damage your health or that of your baby?"

"Of course not!" she snapped angrily. "He would never allow that!"

"But that's exactly what you're doing," he pointed out as tenderly as he could. "All this stress you're under is putting the baby in danger. He's needs all the help he can get to come into this world a healthy little boy, and you're the one who has to make sure he gets that chance. You've got to release this stress. Please, let me help you. Let God help you." He knelt at the altar, happy when she followed his lead. He took her hand in his.

"Roseanna, the victory is yours; just as Jesus spoke peace to the stormy sea, He can speak peace to you; but you've got to allow Him to do it. You've got to turn them loose, you've got to put them in the Father's hands."

"How can I?" she cried. "How can I let go of Brad and my sweet Isabelle? They're the most precious things on earth to me. How can I forget them?"

"You can never forget them," he said, shocked that she had misunderstood what he meant. "That's not what I'm talking about, Roseanna. I'm talking about giving the pain over to God and let him begin the healing process. Only then can you be free of all this hurting inside and the stress it brings."

"But I did that back in Nashville," she said. "I gave my heart to Him and I asked Him to help me, and He did. Why is it necessary to do it again?"

"When you were in Nashville, you had a lot to deal with, the memories, the nightmares, and you got through all of those things; but when you came back here and had to face all the memories in the home you shared with Brad and Isabelle, it started all over again; and the pain was more intense than before, because the memories here are so much more vivid; everywhere you look you see them, and it opens up the wounds again."

"I don't know how to find the faith to trust in God, how to put it in His hands," she said honestly. "Brad has always been my strength; when I lost him, there was nothing left to hold on to."

"I understand," he said. "You've always had someone to lean on, you've never had to learn to lean on God for yourself, someone has always been there to take care of you."

She nodded. "For the first ten years of my life it was my daddy; when he left, Mama took over; then I met Brad and fell in love with him, and he became my strength; when I went to Nashville the first time, the prince and Maurice took care of everything; then God brought Brad and me back together, and I leaned on his faith from then on 'til the day he died..."

"Then I came along and did it again," he blurted out. "God has been trying to give you the faith you need to trust in Him, and I've taken it out of His hands and tried to handle things myself. It made me feel good, thinking I could take care of your problems. Forgive me, Roseanna."

"Andy, you're not going to leave me, are you?" she asked, clinging to him. "I can't make it without you."

"I'm not leaving you, Roseanna, but you can make it without me," he said, holding on to her. "God and you can make it, you don't need me. I don't have the power to make things right in your life; only God can do that."

"Lean on Him---put everything in His hands? I don't know how to do that," she cried.

"We start by asking," he explained. "Father, Roseanna needs You to take control of her life. She needs to learn how to lean on You for comfort and strength. Father, help me step back far enough to let You work; for it's only through You that she can find the peace she so desperately yearns for. I'm sorry, God, that I got in the way of what You were trying to do, and I promise to let You handle things from now on."

They prayed together until a peace came over Roseanna; a peace she didn't understand. The circumstances had not changed; Brad and Isabelle were still gone, the pain of losing them was still there; but a calmness had come over her, and she knew that she could make it now.

"Thank You, Lord," she whispered, as she stood to her feet. "And thank you Andy for being here for me."

"I'll always be here for you," he said, "but your main source of help from now on will be the Lord. And Roseanna, I'm sorry, but I asked you to marry me for all the wrong reasons, so forget everything I said…"

"You don't want us to get married?"

"Of course, I want us to get married, but for the right reasons. I realize now that I took advantage of the situation. I saw that you were vulnerable and my ego got the best of me, making me believe that I must come to your rescue. I proposed to you thinking that you couldn't make it on your own, and I wanted to take care of you. Now, I know you can make it whether I'm with you or not. I still want to take care of you and little Will, but because I love you, not out of need. I want you to marry me because you want to spend the rest of your life with me, not for the reasons I stated before, so I'm starting all over, and I'm asking you, again," he said, taking her hand, and looking into her eyes, "Roseanna, I love you. Will you marry me?"

"I-I don't know, Andy," she stammered. "I've got to sort out my feelings; for you, and, for Brad. I still love him, I always will, and as long as my heart belongs to him…"

"I know you'll always love him," Andy said softly, "but is there room in your heart for another love; a special love that you and I can share together, one that is ours alone, and won't take away from the love you feel for him."

She shook her head. "I don't know," she said again.

"You think it over," he said. "Take as much time as you need. Look inside your heart, get in touch with your deepest feelings; see if there is room for me."

"I will," she promised, "and I'll let you know as soon as possible."

"I'll be waiting," he said. "Oh, by the way, I'm preaching here Sunday morning," he added a bit hesitantly. "Brother Troasclair has another engagement and asked me to fill in for him."

"Andy, that's great," she exclaimed. "Finally, I'll get to hear you preach."

"You don't mind me filling Brad's pulpit?"

"No, I don't mind at all," she said. "I know the church will get a new pastor someday, and I'll have to get used to it, if I'm going to live here."

"That takes a load off my mind," he said. "I'm excited about preaching, but I didn't want to upset you."

"Brad's study books are in his office," she told him. "I've got the key if you would like to use them."

"That would be great, thanks," he said, following her into the office. "Wow, what a library. I've never seen so many books."

Roseanna smiled. "I bought most of them for him the first Christmas I was in Nashville. I had made more money than I ever imagined existed, and I went all out on gifts for everyone, especially Brad."

"Thanks for letting me use these," he said, choosing several books from the shelves.

"I have an ulterior motive," she said laughingly, "I want to hear a good sermon out of you, Sunday." She leaned over and kissed him on the cheek. "I'll go now and let you study. Come by the parsonage when you finish and I'll fix supper for you."

"That sounds wonderful, but call Grandma and let her know," he said. "I don't want to face her wrath if she fixes supper for me and I don't show up."

"You've got that right." Roseanna said, laughing again. "I'll call her first thing."

166

Sunday morning, Andy waited nervously 'til time to preach. Would these people like his style of preaching? His sermons were usually preached in centers to kids, not in churches where most of the congregation are adults. He fiddled with his tie and ruffled through his notes.

"Calm down, you're gonna do great. They're gonna love you," Roseanna leaned over and whispered as she walked to the front for the singing. She sang with a new burst of spirit that she had not felt in a long time; she sang the way she used to, before Brad and Isabelle died. The congregation tried to get into the worship, but the sorrow that hovered over them since Brad's death kept them from really getting free in the spirit.

Andy walked to the pulpit. "Today, I'm going to speak about forgiveness. It's not always easy to forgive, but is it necessary?" He opened his Bible. "Jesus answers that question in the Sermon on the Mount. Turn to Matthew 6: 14-15. Please stand for the reading of God's word," he said, stiffly, trying to be polished and refined. He began to read. "For if you forgive men their trespasses, your heavenly Father will also forgive you: But if you forgive not men their trespasses, neither will your Father forgive your trespasses." He felt awkward standing here, trying to fill this pulpit. His tie was choking him. The suit jacket weighted him down like a suit of armor. Why had he agreed to do this? He hesitated a moment, cleared his throat, then, pulled off his tie and his jacket. He rolled up his sleeves and looked them straight in the eye. "Folks," he began, "I'm going to have to be myself today. I tried to be proper and do everything the correct way, but I was getting nowhere, so I'm going to deliver this message the way God has anointed me to deliver it. I'm not your average dyed-in-the-wool preacher, so if you don't want me to preach, now is the time to say so."

"Preach, brother," the congregation called out in unison.

Roseanna swallowed hard and said a prayer. She had never heard him preach so she didn't know what to expect.

"There are four essential steps to forgiveness," he began. "Three things you don't do and one thing you do. I'm going to use myself as an example, something that happened in my life a few years ago. It's not something I'm proud of, and I'm not proud of the way I handled it, but through it, I learned, the hard way, about forgiveness. When you have been wronged and need to forgive, there are four steps to forgiving, they are:

1. Don't curse it.
2. Don't nurse it.
3. Don't rehearse it.
4. Do disperse it.

First he told them of his experience with someone who had hurt him badly and his reaction to it. He went through each step, acting out his sermon like an actor on the stage.

"First, I cursed the situation by always thinking about the man who had done me wrong, and telling the Lord what a good person I was, and what a rotten person he was. I spent most of my time crying, "Why me, Lord? What have I ever done to deserve this?" He paused.

"After I got through cursing the situation, I nursed it by giving it lots of TLC and making sure it had plenty to feed on; I wasn't going to let it die on me. I nurtured my hurt feelings like a mother her nurtures her baby chicks.

Then I rehearsed it by telling everyone I met how I had been mistreated; I went over and over what had happened to me, with friends and family and anyone who would take the time to listen to my sad tale; and if I couldn't find anyone to listen, I went over it again and again in my own mind, and I even reminded God of how badly I'd been treated, and how the other guy deserved to be punished. I prayed the wrath of God down on his head. But the Lord told me to Shut Up and stop talking about it, to forget the past and look to the future."

The only way I could do this was to Disperse It. Now this was not easy to do. I wanted to hold on to it, because, after all, I was right and the other guy was wrong, so why should I give in? But as I read God's word, I realized that I had to get rid of it. I had to forgive the man...or God wouldn't forgive me."

Roseanna sat there spellbound. The message was not in the slow, deliberate style of Brother Trosclair's sermons, nor the fiery, exciting style of Brad's; but she liked the way he was preaching. What about the rest of the congregation? Did they like it? She looked around. There were smiles on the faces of most of them, some even chuckled out loud. The young people were hanging on to every word. She stole a glance at Deacon LaPree. What was he thinking? He liked staunch, straightforward preaching. She tried to read his face but couldn't. She forced her thoughts back to the message. She didn't want to miss any of it.

Andy expounded in his own unique way, the necessity of forgiving in order to receive forgiveness. He concluded by saying, "If you need to ask someone to forgive you or you need to forgive someone, don't put it off...DO IT RIGHT NOW."

When the service ended and the folks were filing out, they each stopped to shake Andy's hand and tell him how much they enjoyed the message. There was a look of joy on their faces that Roseanna had not seen since...Brad and Isabelle died.

Grandma made her way over to where Ellis LeBlanc was standing. "I need to talk to you," she said, a hint of tears in her eyes. He put his arm around her shoulder and they walked over to a spot out of earshot of the others.

169

"Ellis, I'm sorry for the way I've treated you all these years. Will you forgive me?"

He put his arms around her. "Grandma, you had plenty of reasons to dislike me," he said compassionately. "I'm the one who should be asking for your forgiveness."

And there that day, standing in the little white church, two hearts were cleansed from feelings of hostility that had kept them apart for all these many years, and the two of them were bonded together as a family should be.

Deacon LaPree walked up to Andy and shook his hand. Roseanna held her breath. If there was one thing you could depend on out of the deacon, it was honesty. He wouldn't mince any words. She remembered how rough he'd been on Brad when he first came to pastor the church. Poor Andy, could he take it? She whispered a prayer.

"That was a fine sermon, young man," the deacon commented. "And I like the way you presented it; you got the message over in a way that delighted the folks, and made us laugh; that's what we need in this church, more laughter and good feelings; we've been depressed too long, and I think today broke the ice. I believe we can have a new beginning now."

"Thank you, sir." Andy said, tears misting his eyes as he realized how close he had come to missing the boat, how he had tried to deliver his sermon in a more polished way; the way he thought the people would accept more readily.

Roseanna smiled. "I'll wait for you at the parsonage," she told Andy, as she turned to leave. They were going into town for dinner and she wanted to change into more comfortable shoes.

He nodded. "I'll be there, shortly."

"Will wonders never cease," she remarked later on the way into town. "I never would have believed the good deacon would actually compliment you on the sermon. He

170

usually doesn't take too well to young preachers. It took him forever to warm up to Brad."

Andy had this weird look on his face. "You're not going to believe this," he said. "He asked me to be the new pastor at the church."

"That's wonderful!" she exclaimed. "Are you going to do it?"

"I told him I would pray about it," he said, "but a lot depends on you. How you would feel if I became pastor there. Would you think I was trying to take Brad's place?"

"No, she said. "If you feel like this is right for you, I think you need to do it. I'm glad they have finally found someone they can accept. The church is at a low ebb now without a regular pastor. Brother Trosclaire is good, but he has other obligations and can't devote full time to the church."

She turned the radio on to a station where soft music was playing. They sat quietly listening. "Now for your 1:00 o'clock news," the announcer said. "There is a hurricane brewing out in the Atlantic Ocean. If it stays on course and doesn't lose any of it's velocity, it is estimated to hit the Bahama Islands within two weeks."

Roseanna shivered as a chill ran through her body. "Wow," she said, "it's suddenly so cold in here."

Andy looked at her strangely. "Are you all right?" he asked, "it's not cold in here."

A tear slid down her face. "The last time I felt a chill like that was the day Brad and Isabelle were drown. What could it mean, Andy?"

"The news about the hurricane probably upset you, thinking of the people in its path."

"Yeah, living close to the ocean I know how bad hurricanes can be. I'm sure that's it. We'll pray for the folks in the Bahamas."

The music started playing again. Roseanna closed her eyes and lay back to listen, and to get her thoughts straight.

Andy hummed along with the music.

She raised up. "See that roadside park up ahead," she said, "let's pull over for a minute."

Are you okay?" he asked, concerned about her well-being.

"Yes, I'm fine," she answered getting out of the car.

He got out of the car and walked over to her.

She put her arms around him and pulled him close. She kissed him with all the emotions inside her.

"Wow," he said, "not that I didn't like that kiss, but what's this all about?"

"I just wanted to see what it felt like to kiss you," she said.

"Well?"

"I need more information to render a fair verdict," she said, kissing him again.

He stepped back and held her at arms length. "I'd like nothing better than to stay here and kiss you all afternoon, but I need to know where this is leading."

"I prayed, Andy, but I didn't receive a definite answer," she said, "so I made this decision on my own. I looked in my heart and found there is room for you. I want to marry you, and, for all the right reasons; I love you, and I want to spend the rest of my life with you, that is, if you haven't changed your mind."

This time he grabbed her and kissed her. "Change my mind, not a chance. Roseanna, you've made me the happiest man in the world. I believe you made the right decision. I know God sent me to you in Nashville to help you, so we've got to assume this is His will for our lives. Now, let's set the date."

"If we wait 'til spring, we can go on an extended honeymoon. The baby will be old enough to travel by then..."

"I don't want to wait 'til spring," he said. "I'm thinking more about right now, before the baby is born..."

"I'd have to waddle up the aisle," she protested.

"And no one could do it more beautifully than you," he said, grinning. "All kidding aside, I want to marry you before the baby is born. I want to be there for every minute of his life. I want him to start out having a daddy around, even if it is only a substitute dad. I want to be there for you and him."

"Are you sure?" she asked. "In those first few months, there'll be two a.m. feedings, tons of dirty diapers, and walking the floor when the colic sets in. You sure you want to get in on all of that?"

He laughed. "I don't scare easily, and I don't want to miss out on one minute of raising him; so let's get this show on the road."

"The baby is due in about a month," she mused out loud. "Thanksgiving Day is about three weeks away. How about Thanksgiving afternoon?"

"It's a date," he said.

"We'll have a simple ceremony at the church with just family and close friends," she said. "I don't want a lot of frills, if that's okay with you."

He nodded. "I'd marry you under a shade tree in the middle of an open field, with no one there but us and the minister."

She laughed. It felt good to laugh again. It felt good being here with Andy. "Will your family be coming?" she asked.

"I doubt it," he said, "they're staying close to my brother's bedside until he gets back on his feet. If it's okay with you, we'll visit them later."

"That's fine. Now, let's get going," she said, giving him another kiss. "I'm eating for two now and little Will is starving."

"Big Andy is getting pretty hungry too," he said, helping her in the car.

"After we eat, let's stop by and tell Belle and Jesse the good news," she suggested. "My sister is going to be so happy."

"Do you think they really like me? Do you think they will accept me as your husband?" He was a bit worried. Brad was so perfect, and so adored by all the folks here on the bayou, could he ever measure up to him?

Roseanna read his thoughts. "They like you for who you are," she assured him. "They won't judge you according to Brad's standards."

She snuggled close to him and laid her head on his shoulder. He put his arm around her and held her close. As she sat there in the safety of his arms, for the first time in a long time she felt happy and content.

Chapter 24

Isabelle was excited as she pressed the flowers in the book. Big Jake had let her pick out the book she wanted to put them in. "I want this one with all the pretty pictures," she said, choosing a book of fairy tales. She pressed one rose on the page that had a picture of a beautiful princess. "That looks like Mommy." She rubbed her hand over the face of the princess. "I miss my mommy." A tear slid down her cheeks.

"Kid, we're going to get you back to your mommy as soon as possible," Jake promised, as visions of dismantling his cabin flashed through his mind. Only as a last resort he quickly added to his thoughts.

"Daddy, I've got my flowers in this book," Isabelle exclaimed, as Brad walked in. "Do you want me to put yours in a book too?"

He nodded, handing her the yellow roses.

"Big Jake says we're going home soon," she said, excitedly. "We're going to see Mommy."

"That's great, honey," Brad told her, glancing at Jake.

"Thanksgiving will be here in a couple of months," he said. "I think we should try to have you two home by then."

"Big Jake, you're not coming with us?" Isabelle asked.

"No, kid, I'm gonna stay here," he said.

"Please come home with us," she pleaded. "I don't want to leave you here by yourself."

"Don't worry about me. I'll be fine." He swallowed over the lump in his throat. It was hard saying no to her. It was hard walking away from the love she had for him, an unconditional love; a love that didn't care if his face was disfigured; but she was not the rest of the world; and it was that world and it's cruelty that he had to hide from.

"Daddy, tell Big Jake that he has to come home with us," she said, sure that if her daddy spoke the word it would be done.

"Sweetheart, we'll have to let Jake make that decision," he said gently. "I hope he will change his mind and come with us, but we can't force him to."

"God can make him," she said firmly, "Big Jake I'm gonna pray for you everyday. I'm gonna ask God to make you come home with us."

Big Jake didn't reply to her announcement to pray for him. Instead he picked up his garden tools. "I'm going to work in the garden," he said, "does anyone want to help me?"

"I do," she squealed happily. She loved working in the garden with him, and he had said the watermelons should be ripe any day now. She could hardly wait to dig into the sweet taste of the luscious melons.

Big Jake thumped a few of the big melons. "I think this one is ripe," he said. "Shall we check it out?"

"Yeah," she said, her stomach all tingly with anticipation.

Jake cut the melon from the vine and carried it inside. With a sharp knife he cut it in half. A bright red center told them it was just right for eating. He cut slices for each of them.

"This is the best thing I ever tasted," Isabelle exclaimed joyfully. There were bananas, figs, oranges, and pineapples on the island, but their goodness didn't come close to this. "How many watermelons do we have left?" she asked.

Jake laughed. "We have so many that you'll probably get tired of eating them before they're all gone."

"Look at that big funny looking bird," Isabelle exclaimed the next day as they sat by the water's edge painting. "It's as pink as an Easter egg."

"That's a roseate spoonbill," he explained. "See how he's swinging his bill back and forth through the water. That's the way he eats."

"His mommy sure didn't teach him any table manners," Isabelle said, shaking her head.

"Would you like to learn more about birds?"

She nodded eagerly.

"Let's put our paints away for today, and do some bird watching," he said.

They walked around the island and he pointed out the different kinds of birds that shared the island with them. They saw tiny hummingbirds, flocks of green parrots, white crowned pigeons, and ring-necked pheasants; he also showed her some quail and two kinds of doves. He didn't mention that some of those birds had been on their dinner plates recently; he didn't think she needed to know that. "That's all for today," he said. "It's time to be getting back to the cabin."

"Can we do this again, Big Jake?" she asked eagerly.

"Yeah, we'll do it again tomorrow," he promised, tingling with excitement. It felt good to once again open a child's eyes to the knowledge of the world around them. He felt alive and vibrant as he watched the sparkle in Isabelle's eyes; and to know he helped put it there made him feel that life was worth living.

A month passed. Big Jake had continued to teach Isabelle, not only out of books, but they had followed up on the bird watching, and also scouted the island in hopes of seeing some wild horses and donkeys that sometimes live on these uninhabited islands. One day they caught a glimpse of a raccoon. Isabelle wanted to make a pet of him; but Big Jake talked her out of it.

"There's a Christmas flower," she exclaimed, pointing to a red poinsettia.

"This island is a virtual paradise of flowers," he told her. "Let's see how many we can find."

Isabelle skipped ahead of him, keeping her eyes pealed for different kinds of flowers.

They saw purple bougainvillea, golden allamanda, blue petrea, white and pink frangipani, a deep-red chenille plant as well as several other varieties.

"Big Jake, how do you know so much?" she asked. "Next to my daddy, you must be the smartest man in the world."

"I brought a lot of books about these islands with me when I came here," he said, "and I'd had a lot of time to study all of them."

Brad and Isabelle had church every Sunday and Jake always found excuses to stay away from the services. It was Sunday and Brad had planned the service as usual. His mind was on Roseanna, as it so often was. He wondered where she was; what she was doing. He was sure they had gotten a new pastor at the church by now, so where was she living; had she moved back home with her parents, was she living in town with Belle and Jesse; or had she built the house that they had planned to build one day? "Oh, sweetheart," he whispered, "if only I could know where you are, and how you're doing. I'm so lost without you, Roseanna. I'm trying to be strong for Isabelle's sake, but sweetheart, I'm not strong. When I think about you and how much I love and miss you, it's all I can do to keep from falling to pieces. With every passing day my love for you grows stronger, and the longing in my heart to see you, to hold you, becomes even more unbearable. I've got to get back home to you soon, my darling, or I'll just wither away, for I can't survive much longer without you."

He forced his thoughts back to the service today. If there was only some way he could get Jake to hang around. "Lord, there's got to be a way," he prayed.

Jake walked by just then, fishing pole in hand.

"Big Jake, you going fishing again, instead of coming to church?" Isabelle asked. "I wanted you to hear me sing. I'm singing a song just for you, a song my mommy sings. Won't you please stay so I can sing for you?"

"We'll let her sing first," Brad broke in, "there'll be plenty of time to go fishing afterward."

"Okay, I'll stay 'til she sings," Jake said with a sigh.

"Thank you," Isabelle said, giving him a hug.

Brad walked to the pulpit. "First, we'll pray," he said. "Let's pray for all the folks back home, especially Roseanna; also for us, that God will continue to keep His hand on us."

"Let's pray that Big Jake will want to go home with us, so his mommy won't be sad anymore," Isabelle requested with a heart of sincerity and love. She walked over and took his hand, and began to pray. "God, please watch over mommy and all of us; and please make Big Jake feel better so he will go home with us and his mommy won't sad anymore. Thank you, God," she said, as if it was already done.

When the prayer ended, Isabelle walked up to the pulpit and started singing, in a voice filled with childlike faith and worship.

"Amazing Grace, how sweet the sound,
That saved a wretch like me;
"I once was lost, but now I'm found,
Was blind, but now I see.

'Twas Grace that taught my heart to fear,

179

And Grace that fear relieved;
How precious did that Grace appear,
The hour I first believed.

Through many dangers, toils and snares,
I have already come;
'Twas Grace that brought me safe thus far,
And Grace will lead me home".

Big Jake wiped away tears running down his face as Isabelle sang. Brad walked over and put his arm around his shoulder. He invited Jake to pray.

"The Lord is standing with outstretched arms beckoning to you to come home to Him," he told him.

Jake fell to his knees. "Lord, I'm sorry for staying away from you all these years. Please forgive me and take me back," he prayed. "I want to be a part of Your family again."

They prayed until a smile came across Jake's face. "Thank You, Lord," he said, "I'm so happy to be back in Your family. Now, Lord, give me the wisdom to know what to do, and the grace to do it. I want my life to count for You."

"Since you're not sad anymore, are you going back home with us," Isabelle asked excitedly.

"We'll have to wait and see," he answered, still not sure if he was ready to face the outside world again.

After dinner, they walked along the beach. Isabelle hunted for seashells; Big Jake took his paints and canvas along to paint; but Brad's thoughts were on Roseanna. He felt certain they would be going home soon; their work on the island was finished, now that Jake had given his heart to the Lord. "Sweetheart," he whispered, as if she were standing there beside him, "it won't be long until we're back in each others arms."

Brad stood gazing out over the vast ocean; the same waters that had taken him away from his beloved Roseanna would soon carry him back to her. His heart leapt with joy as he thought of seeing her again, holding her in his arms and kissing her. A cloud overshadowed his heart. "Roseanna, sweetheart," he whispered again, sensing that something was wrong. Panic seized him. "Lord, keep her safe, and take us back to her soon." Little did he realize that at that very moment, back home on the bayou, Roseanna was in the arms of another man, and making plans to marry him.

During the next week, Brad and Big Jake went over plans to get off the island. Since Jake didn't know if he was going with them, they didn't consider tearing down the cabin to build a raft. The plans were going slow without the proper equipment to build the raft.

Thursday, a week before Thanksgiving, dawned clear and fair. The sky over the ocean was blue with fleecy clouds scattered across it. The air was damp and salty; it could have been just another late fall day on the island. But by evening the wind and sea were rising.

Jake paced along the beach. Worry lines wrinkled his forehead. "I don't like the looks of this," he told Brad when they were out of earshot of Isabelle.

"What's wrong," Brad asked, a worried look on his face.

"I'm not sure, but we'd better get prepared for the worst," he said. "I've studied a lot about hurricanes and unless I miss my guess, I'd say one is headed this way."

"What can we do?" Brad had been close enough to these deadly storms to know the grave danger they were in if Jake was right. "I know the best thing is to evacuate, but since we can't do that, what else can we do?"

"Well, we don't have any way to communicate with the outside world, so we know nothing about the storm; if there is one; we don't know how fast it is traveling; how hard the winds are blowing, and how high the waves are. We need to prepare for both wind and the water that might come with it."

"Hurricane Camille that hit the Gulf coast in 1969 had storm surges with a wall of water at least 19 ft. high," Brad stated, having heard stories from his family in Mississippi about how badly Pass Christian had been hit by the storm. "We won't stand a chance if water that high comes onto the island. Our only hope is to pray for God's protection."

"There are some things we can do," Jake said. "We can make everything as secure as possible. There is a small cave-like opening in the rocks on the other side of the island; that will shield us from the wind, but if the high water comes..."

"We'll have to pray that it doesn't," Brad interrupted, not wanting to think of that possibility.

"We need to store as many supplies in the cave as possible," Jake said.

"Let's do that right now," Brad said, anxious to do everything within their power to keep them safe. They would have to depend on God for the things they couldn't do.

There was enough daylight left for them to gather the supplies and take them to the cave. "Hopefully, we won't need this," Jake commented, "but just in case the storm does hit, we'll be ready."

Brad and Jake took turns sleeping and standing watch that night. The winds grew stronger and the waves were dashing against the reefs. By morning it was evident by the mass of dark clouds off on the horizon, that something was going on out in the Atlantic Ocean. They prayed again for God's protection.

It was mid-afternoon and they watched what appeared to be big bands of fog rolling in over the ocean. "Run to the cave!" Jake shouted. "That's not fog, that's water!"

They hurried to the cave and the men put Isabelle behind them to protect her as much as possible if the water did come. They had barely gotten settled in the cave when the hurricane stuck with all its fury.

The 130 miles per hour winds, sometimes shrieking; sometimes growling like a rushing freight train, bore down on the island. Howling winds toppled trees. The water surged over the island, taking with it everything in its path.

"Daddy, I'm scared!" Isabelle screamed. "Hold me!"

Brad gathered his daughter into his arms. "It's okay, baby," he said, trying to reassure her, "God's watching over us." He knew that was true, but his heart pounded furiously, as the storm raged around them.

Jake could see out of the cave's opening. Palm trees swayed to the ground under the high winds. Birds trying to escape seemed to be flying backwards. "God help us," he prayed at the gruesome sight.

They huddled together, holding hands and praying, as they listened to the fury outside. Suddenly the wind calmed down and silence filled the air; the skies became dry. Isabelle let out a whoop of delight and bolted out of the cave.

"It's over!" she yelled with delight, happy to be out of the small, dark place.

Big Jake rushed out, grabbed her and pulled her back inside the cave. "It's not over," he said. "This is the eye of the storm, there's more to come."

He had barely finished speaking when the second half of the storm hit. This time the winds blew from the opposite direction, doing more havoc, as it howled its way back across the island. Finally, after what seemed like an eternity, the storm passed over and only torrential rains remained.

"We need to stay here 'til morning," Jake told them. "It's too dark now to try to find our way back to the cabin." *If there is still a cabin left to go back to,* he thought.

They lit the candles they had brought, and opened up some cans of food. They had plenty of water and fruit juice to drink while they waited for the light of dawn. Isabelle finally slept resting in her daddy's lap.

The next morning with the coming of day, they left the cave to survey how much damage had been done. As they walked through the tangled mess of what once had been an island paradise, tears misted their eyes.

Isabelle wept when she saw raccoons, birds, and wild hogs lying scattered over the island. "Daddy, why do storms have to come?" she cried. "Why did all these animals have to die?"

Brad shook his head. He couldn't answer her question. He didn't understand why some things happened.

Jake gasped as they came to where the cabin used to be. Only debris remained. They stood there, silently taking it all in. Finally, Jake spoke. "Now, I don't have to decide whether or not to stay on the island, that decision has been made for me."

Brad nodded. "It looks like most of the food supply on the island is gone, and probably most of your supplies, too," he said, as they started moving planks and debris away to see what was beneath the rubble.

The storm had taken its toll. They found a few canned goods still in tact, along with some bottles of water, but for the most part, everything was ruined. The garden, along with most of the other vegetation on the island was laying in a twisted, tangled mess.

"We need to look around for anything we can use to build a raft," Jake said. "We've got to get off this island as soon as possible."

"Is another storm coming?" Isabelle asked, her eyes wide with fright.

"No, kid," Big Jake assured her, "but with all the death here, the air on this island is not going to be fit to breathe."

They scouted the island to see what they could find that might help them build a raft. The storm had washed up several big logs. "Good, we can use these," Jake said. "We can place the logs underneath the planks from the cabin to keep them above the water," Jake said. "That way, both us and our supplies will stay dry."

They got the hammer and nails that they had stored in the cave and carried the planks, that had come through the storm in one piece, to the beach; they gathered the logs together, and started working on the raft.

They had no instructions to go by, so they had to use common sense, and the hit and miss method; they had to keep trying until they found something that worked.

"I wish I could remember how Huck Finn did it," Brad commented. "I must have read that book a dozen times when I was a kid."

"I think every boy has read that book," Jake said, "but I don't remember how he did it either."

They laid the logs lengthwise and nailed the planks running in the opposite direction, on top of the logs.

"This should work," Jake surmised, hoping it would turn out the way he saw it in his head.

They spent the days working on the raft and the nights huddled together in the cave. Their food supply was getting low, so they had to work fast; but they also had to make sure they had a raft that was safe enough to withstand several days on the water in case they weren't picked up right away.

Late on Monday before Thanksgiving they finished a raft that they thought would work. "We need to check it out, before we actually set sail in it," Jake said. "I'll give it a trial run."

They piled rocks on the raft that would equal approximately their weight, and the weight of the food and water they would carry with them. Big Jake shoved off from the bank and carefully steered the raft around the reefs and into the deeper waters. A yell of excitement went up as the raft floated easily under the weight that was on it. Big Jake guided it back to shore and he and Brad pulled it back onto the beach.

"We'll load all the supplies on it tonight," Jake said, "then, tomorrow, early, we'll get started on our journey home."

An utter of praise went forth from Brad's lips. "Thank You, Father," he exclaimed. Tears misted his eyes as thankfulness filled his heart. They were finally going home; home to Roseanna; how good that sounded. "Thank You, Lord," he whispered again.

The sun was shining brightly the next morning when they awoke. Excitement filled the air; this was the day they had been waiting for. They hurried to the beach. The men put the raft into the water, holding on to it to make sure it didn't get away from them.

Brad took Isabelle's hand to help her on the raft. "No, daddy, no," she cried. "I don't want to get back in the water. I'm scared."

"Sweetheart," Brad said, gently, "we have to get on this raft; it's the only way we can get back home to mommy. Please, don't be afraid. God is watching over us."

"Okay," she said, trembling, but trying to be brave. "I want to see Mommy, so I'll go, but hold on to me tightly, daddy, don't let me fall in the water again."

"Oh, sweetheart, Big Jake and I will both watch over you, day and night, we'll make sure you don't fall in the water." He climbed on the raft with her and held her trembling body in his arms.

"Are we all set?" Big Jake asked, then pushed the raft away from the shore and steered it again into the deep water. He climbed on board and he and Brad took turns paddling to keep the raft going in the right direction.

Isabelle finally calmed down and fell asleep as the sun's warm rays beat down upon them.

"Jake," Brad began, "when we're rescued where will you be going? You want to come home with us?"

"No, I'm going home to Texas," he replied. "I'm going to see my mother."

"She'll be so happy to see you," Brad said, thinking of the happy reunion between mother and son.

"I'll be happy to see her, too," Jake said. "Being away from her was the hardest part of being on the island."

"When we get back to civilization, I have plenty of money for all of us," Brad said, glad that Roseanna had insisted he take twice the amount of money he'd need for the fishing trip. "So don't worry about the expense of getting home."

"Thanks, I didn't carry money with me when I went to the island. I never intended to leave. But now that the Lord has come into my life, I'm excited about going home."

"If you still wish to have the cosmetic surgery, remember, we will pay all your bills, that's the least we can do after all you've done for us," Brad told him.

"I probably will have it done," Jake said. "I want to get back into teaching, and I will need a new face for that.

But, now that I've got the Lord to sustain me, I won't mind facing the jeers until I get it done."

Tears misted Brad's eyes as he thought of the difference God had made in Jake's life. He had gone from a man with no hope to one with a bright future. "Thank you, Lord," he whispered gratefully.

The hours dragged slowly by. The sun beat down on them during the daylight hours; at night their only light was a battery-operated lantern. They had been on the water for two days and had not seen even a hint of anything resembling a ship. Darkness surrounded them for the second time since they left the island. The men tried to stay awake, but weariness overcame them and they dropped off to sleep.

"Today is Thanksgiving," Brad remarked the next morning.

"Will we be home in time to eat at Grandma's house?" Isabelle asked, happily.

"I sure hope so," Brad answered, "we'll have to wait and see. It depends on how quickly someone finds us."

Isabelle closed her eyes and looked upward. "God, please let someone find us in time so we can get to Grandma's house and eat turkey and dressing and chocolate pie," she prayed earnestly.

"Chocolate pie?" Jake asked, raising his eyebrows. "I thought it was pumpkin pie for Thanksgiving."

Brad laughed. "Grandma makes pumpkin pies too, several of them. But the kids love her chocolate pies, so she also makes them on every special occasion."

"She cooks the best in the world," Isabelle bragged.

"Your grandma sounds like a great lady," Jake said. "I hope I can meet her someday."

"You can come home with us and eat Thanksgiving dinner," Isabelle offered.

"I'm going home to see my mother," he told her.

A smile covered her face. "Your mommy won't be sad, anymore, Big Jake."

Brad's heart was filled to overflowing, but there were apprehensions too. What if they didn't make it home in time for Thanksgiving dinner. How disappointed Isabelle would be. What if they didn't get home at all? He looked out over the vast waters that surrounded them. They were only a little speck out here on this mighty ocean. If a ship came by, would the folks on it even see them?

For the eyes of the Lord run to and fro throughout the whole earth, to show himself strong in behalf of them whose heart is perfect toward him. Brad nodded in understanding as this familiar scripture came to his mind. How often he had leaned on it, and now when he needed it most, God had brought it to his remembrance. He no longer had any doubts; God was watching over them, and they would make it home; maybe not in time for Thanksgiving; but they would make it home safely. "Thank You, Father," he whispered.

"Daddy! Big Jake! Isabelle yelled. "Look, there's a boat!"

The two men looked, and off on the horizon there was a boat, and it was coming straight toward them.

"Thank You, God," they exclaimed, as tears ran down their faces. They were going home!

Chapter 25

Thanksgiving Day dawned clear and brisk on the bayou. Roseanna awoke early. Today was her wedding day. Her heart should be filled with happiness; and it was to some degree; but there was also a deep down sadness as she thought of another wedding, seven years ago, the day she became Mrs. Bradley Lefourche. Today, she would give up that name forever. Could she bear to do that? She poured a cup of coffee from the coffeemaker that she had set the night before to automatically brew and be ready when she awoke. Tears stung her eyes. "Brad," she whispered. She finished the cup of coffee and poured more into a large thermal mug. She grabbed a sweater and headed out into the briskness of the November day. She walked to her special place. She felt close to Brad here. She had to be alone with him one more time.

She sat down on the log where they had sat the first day she'd met him. She rubbed her hand over the log as tears filled her eyes and blinded her. She wiped the tears on the sleeve of her sweater. Her throat burned, her heart ached to see him one more time, to feel his arms around her and taste the sweetness of his kiss. "Oh, Brad, my darling, I will always love you, nothing on earth could ever change that. If I could only go back, I would never have let you and Isabelle go on that fishing trip without me, for I had rather be with you in death than to live on this earth without you. But, for some reason, God chose to take you and to leave me here..." More tears flooded her eyes.

"Today, is my wedding day, Brad, and as I stand on the brink of giving my heart to another man, my thoughts are consumed with you and the love we shared. In a few hours I will covenant before God, to love another man for the rest of my life. How can I do that when my heart is still filled with love for you, and always will be. I love him, not in the way I love you, but I do love him. He's a wonderful man; he's more like you than anyone I've ever met. He has brought sunshine into my life when there was nothing but darkness ahead for me. I know I'm doing the right thing by marrying him, but it's so hard to let you go." More tears ran down her face.

"Brad, in a few days, you and I will have a son. The son we wanted so badly, the son we prayed for, the son that will carry on your name for generations to come. I'm so thankful that I will always have a part of you here with me; you will live on through him. I will make sure the love we shared lives on in him, and he will be able to feel your love reaching out to him even though you can't be here for him. I ask for your guidance to always hover over him, for there's times when he will need his father's wisdom. Oh, my darling, if only..." She tried to compose herself. "Brad, I want you to know that Andy will be a good substitute father. He will never take your place, I'd never allow that; and he would never try. I searched my heart, Brad, before I decided to marry Andy; and I decided to marry him for several reasons; I do love him as much as I can ever love anyone other than you, and I don't want to raise our son in an atmosphere of gloom and sadness; it wouldn't be good for him to live that way. Andy will give us a life of happiness and love. He will make sure Will grows into the kind of man you could be proud of; and that's one of the reasons I love him. He's a good man, Brad. I wouldn't trust just anyone to raise your son." Her heart was breaking inside her.

"Brad, I've come to the most difficult time in my life; when I must do the hardest thing I've ever done; I've got to say goodbye to you. I've got to tuck away the precious memories of you into a special place in my heart, and keep them there, only to be remembered now and then. From this moment forward, I can't allow my thoughts to be consumed with you, and the love I feel for you; that wouldn't be fair to Andy. When I pledge myself to him today, it must be all of me; anything less would be a mockery to the holy bonds of marriage."

She slowly pulled off her wedding band, the one Brad had slipped on her finger the day they became man and wife. She unclasped the locket that he had given her, which had also been a symbol of their love, and took it from around her neck. She placed the wedding band on the chain with the locket and clasped them in her hand. She held them to her bosom and wept. "Goodbye, my love," she whispered, kissing the ring and the locket, as tears rolled down her face. She jumped up and ran toward the parsonage, her eyes stinging, her throat burning from breathing in the crisp air; and her heart broke inside her.

"Belle, am I doing the right thing?" she asked later as her sister was helping her get ready for the wedding.

"Do you have doubts about Andy?" Belle asked, worried that Roseanna would still not be sure of her feelings for the man she would be marrying in a couple of hours.

"No, I don't have doubts about him. I'm sure I love him," Roseanna said, "but my heart is still filled with love for Brad, and I think it always will be."

"Roseanna, the love you and Brad had was special, a once in a lifetime kind of love, you will never forget it, and you will never love another man the way you loved him, but he's gone, honey. You've got to move on, and if you're sure that Andy is the man you want to spend the rest of your life with, the love that you two share will take care of these other things."

"Thanks, Belle, I needed to hear that," Roseanna said, wiping the tears away. "I went to my special place this morning to say goodbye to Brad, and it took all the strength within me to let him go. I want to marry Andy, but it's so hard letting go of the past, and the love Brad and I shared."

"I know, sweetie," Belle said, holding her sister, and weeping for a perfect love that was lost forever. She didn't know what she would do if she ever lost Jesse.

Roseanna had chosen a cream colored gown, styled in simple lines, with mauve accessories. A cascade of tiny mauve roses adorned the simple veil. She would carry a bouquet of mauve tipped roses.

Belle, her only attendant, would march up the aisle wearing a mauve colored gown, made along the same simple lines of the bride's gown.

They fixed each other's hair and got dressed with still a half hour or so to go before the ceremony. They waited in the parsonage until time for the ceremony to begin.

Andy awoke that morning with thoughts of what today held. He was taking a big step here. A step he had not been willing to take since Emily. Could he give his heart and his love to this woman who would soon become his wife? He had never loved anyone completely except Emily. He had gone back home the first part of the week to say goodbye to her. As he knelt and placed red roses on her grave, it seemed as if he could once again hear her laughter, feel her warm kisses and hear her say; "Andy, I love you." Tears rolled down his face. Could he ever love anyone the way he loved her? Was it fair to pledge himself to another, with thoughts of Emily still in his heart? He wanted to marry Roseanna and spend the rest of his life with her; but first he had to deal with the memories of the past. "Emily," he began. "I love you as much today as I did the day I married you. I could never love you any less; you will always have a special place in my heart and I will cherish your memory forever, but, sweetheart, I've come here today to say goodbye. For the first time since I lost you, I've found someone else that I can love. Her name is Roseanna and I'm going to marry her. She's a lot like you, she makes me laugh, and feel happy inside, the way you always did. I've felt empty and hollow inside since I lost you, but Roseanna has filled that void in my life. Emily, my darling, the one thing I regret most of all is that I never went to church with you. I could have made your life so much happier had I shared your love for God and your church. I know that wherever you are, you will be proud that finally your prayers have been answered, and I am now serving the God that you loved so much. I will never forget you, my darling, but I must say goodbye to you, now, for when I pledge my love to Roseanna, there must be no restraints on that love." He kissed the tips of his fingers and ran them across her name on the tombstone. "Goodbye,_my sweet Emily," he whispered and ran down the hill.

Now, on the morning of his wedding day, he wiped a tear away as he thought back to saying goodbye to Emily. How hard it had been. Then his thoughts turned to Roseanna. She couldn't go to Brad's grave and say goodbye to him, today, on the day she would become another man's wife. How she must be feeling. As painful as it was, going to Emily's grave and saying goodbye, he found a certain amount of solace by being able to do it. Roseanna didn't have that comfort. "God help her," he prayed.

Roseanna and Daddy stood just outside the door that led to the sanctuary. Belle was walking up the aisle to take her place in front of the altar. In a few minutes, the pianist would begin playing the wedding march, and Roseanna would take the first step into her new life, as she started up the aisle to Andy, who was waiting there for her.

"Roseanna, are you sure about this?" Ellis LeBlanc asked, a worried look on his face, as he saw the tears that were misting her eyes.

"Oh, Daddy, I love him, but I don't know if I can do this," she cried. "How can I promise myself to another man standing in the same spot where Brad and I stood when we took our vows."

Strains of "Here Comes The Bride" drifted throughout the sanctuary. Ellis LeBlanc took his daughter's arm. "Now's the time to call this off, if you're not absolutely sure," he said. "You don't have to go through with it."

The wedding guests turned to look at the doors, expecting them to open and Roseanna to walk through. But the doors didn't open. Belle stared at the closed doors. What was going on? She stole a glance at Andy. He was looking at the doors with a bewildered look on his face.

Outside, Roseanna stood frozen in place. Her feet wouldn't carry her forward. "Daddy I want to marry him," she said. "I love him and I can't imagine my life without him. It's just so hard, so many memories of Brad..."

"I know, baby," he said, a tear trickling down his face. "I loved Brad like a son. No one can ever take his place, and I understand how you must feel today. Andy is a fine young man too, and I believe he loves you."

"Daddy, help me," she said.

"Do I go in and make the announcement, or do we go in together?" he asked, opening the door.

She slipped her arm through his. "We go in together," she said, stepping through the door. "Just stay close, Daddy."

Everyone stood, smiling, as they saw her walk through the door. They were all still grieving over the loss of Brad and Isabelle, but they liked Andy, and they were glad that Roseanna was getting another chance at happiness.

Roseanna held tightly to her father's arm. She felt like she was going to faint. Was this a mistake? Was it fair to marry Andy when her thoughts were on Brad and the vows they had made here seven years ago. She thought she had put the past to rest this morning in her special place when she had said goodbye to Brad, but now... Oh, if only she could talk to Andy and tell him how she feels. But it was too late to talk. If she didn't marry him today, she never would, and she would lose him forever. She'd already lost one love, she couldn't stand to lose another. They arrived at the front of the church and stopped.

"Who gives this woman to be married?" Brother Troasclair asked.

"Her mother and I do," Ellis LeBlanc answered, squeezing Roseanna's hand. He leaned over and whispered in her ear: "It's not too late."

She embraced him and whispered back to him. "I'm okay now, Daddy, and I'm sure about this."

He placed her hand into Andy's hand. His touch was strong but gentle. Rosseanna smiled at the man who would soon be her husband.

"If anyone knows any reason why these two should not be joined together in the Holy bonds of matrimony, let him speak now or forever hold his peace." Brother Trosclair said. A hush filled the room. "The rings," he stated. Jesse handed the ring to Andy.

Andy took Roseanna's hand. He looked into her eyes and smiled lovingly at her. He slipped the ring on her finger. "With this ring, I thee wed..."

Chapter 26

Brad, Big Jake and Isabelle waved their arms and yelled at the top of their lungs as the boat came closer and closer to them.

"It's the Coast Guard!" Brad exclaimed.

The boat pulled up beside them and stopped. The men on the boat reached out and pulled them safely onboard.

"How long have you been out here?" the captain asked.

"We've been on this raft for two days," Brad said. "My daughter and I have been stranded on an island for about eight months." He told him the whole story.

The captain smiled. "The world's going to be glad to hear this news; we've all grieved right along with Roseanna," he said. "I'll get in touch with the local TV station..."

"Sir, please don't do that," Brad said, pleadingly. "I want Roseanna to be the first to know that we're alive, and I don't want to tell her over the phone. Give us time to get home, and then release the news."

"I see your point, son," the captain said. "No one else will know who you are, and we'll get you home as soon as possible."

"Thank you, sir," Brad said, gratefully.

"I'm not sure how soon we can get you home," the captain remarked. "Today is Thanksgiving and the airports will be swamped with holiday travelers."

"I'll charter a private jet," Brad told him. "We want to get home in time to eat Thanksgiving dinner with our family."

"That may not be so easy," the captain said. "Most of the pilots for the private jets don't work on holidays unless they are chartered in advance. But I'll try."

"I understand," Brad said with a sigh. "We appreciate all you're doing. We'll need the plane to take Isabelle and me to New Orleans first, and then take Jake on to Houston, Texas. "

The captain nodded. "You must be starving," he said. "What would you like to eat? I'll radio ahead and have some food waiting when we get to shore."

"Hamburger and fries," Isabelle piped up, "and a chocolate milkshake," she added.

"That's what I want too," Big Jake put in.

"That sounds good to me, also," Brad said. "Make it double on the hamburgers and fries, and the biggest milkshakes possible. It's been much too long since we've had a treat like this."

The captain placed the order and requested that a private jet be chartered as soon as possible. "Now, sit back and rest, it'll be a while before we get to Florida.

"How did you find us?" Brad asked.

"We got an anonymous tip, saying that a raft with two adults and a child was spotted somewhere in this region last night, so we set out early this morning in search of you."

"Wonder why they didn't give us a ride back to shore?" Brad mused aloud.

"We figure it was kids who 'borrowed' a boat for a joy ride. They didn't give us their names, but said they saw a light out in the middle of the ocean and cut their motor, and went in for a closer look, that's when they saw the raft and what looked like two adults and a child on board. We thought maybe it was a prank, but we look into every report that comes in, prank or not."

"Thank God, you found us," Brad said.

They settled down for the ride back to Florida. This was the first leg of their journey home. Isabelle sat in the captain's chair, wearing his cap, steering the boat, and asking every question imaginable. By the time they docked, she would know all there was to know about piloting a boat.

"I've been on the radio and they have found a private jet for you, but the pilot is visiting relatives in another town, so it will take him a couple of hours to get to the airport," the captain reported a little while later. "We're about thirty minutes away from the harbor so you will have at least an hour and half before you can fly out. I can call ahead and reserve a room for you at a local hotel if you want to freshen up before your trip home."

"What about clothes?" Brad asked. "Is there a place open today where we can buy clothes and the other things we'll need to freshen up."

The captain rubbed his chin and thought a minute. "There's a hotel that has all kinds of shops in it and they're open everyday. You should find what you need there," he said. "I'll make reservations for you and also have your food waiting when you check in. I'll explain the situation as best I can, without telling them who you are."

"Thanks," Brad said. "How can we ever repay you for all your kindness?"

"Just getting you home is payment enough," the captain said, his voice choking. "I was part of the team who searched for you and your little girl eight months ago. I heard the pain in your wife's voice, begging me to find you and bring you back home to her. Those words have haunted me ever since, wondering if we did everything we could have done. I'm thankful you're alive and well, and that we were able to find you this time."

They went straight to the hotel when they docked in the harbor in Florida.

"This is the best stuff I ever tasted," Isabelle exclaimed, cramming the burger and fries into her mouth. "And the best chocolate milkshake," she added.

"Slow down, baby," Brad admonished her. "You'll make yourself sick." He knew how she felt; he had to fight the urge to stuff the food into his mouth.

They went shopping as soon as they finished eating. Jake didn't want to go out, so, Brad got his sizes and bought clothes for him. He let Isabelle choose her outfit. She looked through all the dresses, finally choosing a bright pink one. They got a pair of sandals to match the dress; blue jeans and pullover shirts for Brad and Jake; then went to the toiletry department and bought the other things they needed, including a hairbrush for Isabelle.

They hurried back to the room to get ready. While Isabelle was showering, Brad made a couple of phone calls. He called the airport in New Orleans and made arrangements to have a rental car waiting when the plane landed.

He'd realized he didn't know where Roseanna would be. He felt sure, after this amount of time, they had gotten a new pastor at the church so she would no longer be living in the parsonage. Where would she be? Had she moved back in with her parents? Was she living with Belle and Jesse in town, or had she built the dream house they had planned to build? He needed to know exactly where to find her so he could be sure that she would be the first to know that he and Isabelle were alive. He would call her parents house and, disguising his voice he'd ask where she was. He dialed the number and waited.

"Hello," a child's voice answered.

Brad smiled. Lee had answered the phone. He wouldn't realize who was calling. "Can you tell me where Roseanna is?" he asked casually.

"She went to the church to marry Andy and then they went to the hospital to get the baby," Lee answered, just as casually.

Brad dropped the phone. The color drained from his face. He couldn't believe the words he'd just heard. Roseanna---married---a baby; what did it mean? He stood there in a daze.

"Bad news?" Jake asked, seeing the look of horror on Brad's face.

Brad nodded. "It seems as if Roseanna got married today, and is at the hospital right now having a baby."

"How can that be?" Jake said. "Maybe, you misunderstood."

"I don't think so," Brad said. "I don't want Isabelle to know about this until I find out for sure what's going on," he added. "It would break her heart."

"She won't hear it from me," Jake promised.

Isabelle came bounding into the room. "I got dressed all by myself. See my pretty dress," she exclaimed, twirling around like a fairy princess. "Daddy, will you brush my hair?"

Brad composed himself. "Sweetheart, Daddy's got to shower and get dressed. It's almost time to leave. I'll brush your hair on the plane."

"Big Jake, will you help me put my shoes on?"

"Sure, kid, and I'll run this comb through your hair to get the tangles out," he said, pulling the comb gently through her wet hair. "That way it will be easier for your daddy to brush it later."

Later, on the plane, Isabelle chattered like a magpie, while Brad brushed her hair. He usually hung on to her every word, but now he didn't hear a word she said. It was hard to concentrate when his mind, his thoughts, his entire being was consumed with Roseanna. How could she have married someone else? Their love was going to last throughout eternity; had she forgotten him in eight short months? And what about the baby? Roseanna would have had to turn to another man shortly after the accident in order to be having a baby now. The baby would be premature even at that. What if the baby died---what would that do to Roseanna, so soon after losing Isabelle? "God, watch over the baby and Roseanna," he prayed silently. He couldn't bear the thought of her going through even more pain.

Jake saw the distress Brad was in, and surmised that he needed to be alone with his thoughts. "Come here, kid, let me brush your hair," he said. "I think your daddy needs to rest. He's got a long drive ahead of him when the plane lands."

Brad lay back in the seat and closed his eyes, but he didn't rest. His thoughts were dark, unsettling. Had Lee gotten the facts wrong? Had Roseanna gone to *a* wedding at the church and then on to the hospital where *someone* was having a baby?

Maybe Angelina had found the right guy and they had gotten married. That could have happened in the eight months they were gone. After all, the LeBlanc girls were not known for long engagements. He was just fretting for no reason. What were Lee's exact words when he asked where he could find Roseanna. *"She went to the church to marry Andy, then they went to the hospital to get the baby."* That didn't sound as if it were just any wedding---Roseanna did marry a guy named Andy. Who was he and where did they meet? And how could she fall in love with him so quickly? Was he a con artist after her money? She would have been gullible after what she'd gone through. *Wait 'til I get my hands on him,* Brad thought. He must be the baby's father, and that meant that he took advantage of Roseanna's grief right after the accident. But, what if she loved him? What if he were the man she wanted in her life now? Brad's heart broke inside him. How could he face the rest of his life without Roseanna?

"Mr. Lefourche, we're getting ready to land in New Orleans," the pilot announced over the intercom. "Please secure everything and fasten your seatbelts."

"Daddy, we're almost home," Isabelle squealed. "We'll see Mommy soon. Will she be glad to see us?"

"Yes, angel, Mommy will be very glad to see us," he assured her.

They said tearful goodbyes to Big Jake and went directly to the car rental booth. In a matter of minutes they were on the highway that led to the bayou, to home. Brad's thoughts were again troubled. What would home be like now with Roseanna married to someone else?

"Is Mommy at our house, daddy?" Isabelle asked, breaking into his thoughts.

"No, honey, Mommy is at the hospital."

"Is Mommy going to die?" Isabelle asked, a look of terror in her eyes.

"No, baby, Mommy will be all right," he said, weighing his words carefully. "We'll be there in a little while and you can see for yourself."

"I can't wait to see Mommy," she said. "I don't ever want to get lost from her again."

Isabelle chatted on and on about Roseanna. Brad could sense by the hunger in her voice how much she longed to see her mother again. It matched the hunger in his heart to see Roseanna, to hold her in his arms and kiss her sweet lips. Tears misted his eyes as each hum of the engine brought them closer to the one he loved more than life itself; and, to whatever was waiting when he got there.

Chapter 27

Brad's heart leapt with joy as he and Isabelle stepped into Roseanna's hospital room. She looked like an angel, lying there, sleeping, her long brown hair, covering the pillow. She had never looked more beautiful to him.

"Isabelle, stay here, and let me wake Mommy gently," Brad whispered. "We don't want to scare her." He walked over and kissed her tenderly.

"Andy," Roseanna mumbled, opening her eyes. A gasp of horror came from her lips, when she saw Brad standing there. "No, no, not the nightmares again," she cried, in a muffled voice as she backed away from him. Her eyes flitted wildly as she looked at the mirage before her.

Isabelle heard her mother's voice and ran to the bed. "Mommy! Mommy!" she squealed happily jumping on the bed. "I love you, Mommy. I love you, and I missed you," she exclaimed, kissing Roseanna again and again.

"Oh, God, please, not the nightmares," Roseanna whimpered, "I can't stand any more nightmares..."

"Sweetheart, this is not a dream, we're alive," Brad said, taking her in his arms and pulling her close.

Isabelle didn't understand what was going on. "Mommy, do you still love us?" she cried. "Are you glad to see us?"

Roseanna trembled as uncontrollable sobs shook her body.

Brad took her hands and rubbed them across his face. "Feel us, sweetheart, we're real flesh and blood, we're alive, and we've come back to you."

Roseanna felt his face, then Isabelles. "You feel real, but the nightmares are real, too," she sobbed. "You're in the ocean and I almost make it to you; then you disappear into the raging waters, there are sharks and blood..." She hesitated a moment. "I can't stand any more nightmares..."

"Oh, my precious Roseanna," Brad cried, encircling her and Isabelle in his arms, "what you must have gone through. There'll be no more nightmares, I promise. God has brought us back to you."

"I'm not dreaming? You're really here, you're alive?" she muttered feebly, her hands trembling, afraid to believe that this was real. "But how? Jesse searched for you; the Coast Guard searched for days, and I hired searchers for months, and none of them found even a trace of you..."

"God picked us up out of the water in His big hands and carried us to an island and we stayed there 'til the storm came," Isabelle explained.

Roseanna looked at Brad. He nodded, and told her the whole story. How he had jumped in the water to save Isabelle; how the raging waters had swept them away before Jesse could reach them; how he had grabbed a log that floated by, and held on for hours, holding on to the log with one arm and Isabelle with the other. "Then everything went black, and I don't remember anything until I came to on the island," he explained. "Isabelle will have to tell you what happened after I passed out."

"It was dark and Daddy let go of me and I fell down under the water. I was so scared. I couldn't breathe. I cried for Daddy to help me. Then, these big hands picked me up out of the water and I could breathe again, and I fell asleep. Daddy woke me up and we were on this island. Daddy said it was God's hands that got us out of the water."

"Thank you, Father, thank You," Roseanna cried as the three of them clung to each other, embracing hungrily, tears of joy flowing down their faces. "God answered my prayer," she said, and told them how she had gone to her special place when Daddy and Jesse got home that night, and told her about the accident. "I fell on my knees before God. I knew He could see you, that you were not lost to Him, and I asked Him to please pick you up out of those waters and bring you back to me." Her voice faltered. "That's exactly what He did." She hesitated momentarily. "I'm so ashamed. When a week passed and there was no sight of you, I thought God had let you die alone out in that ocean; that He had totally forsaken you and I hated Him..."

"You hated God," Isabelle blurted out in surprise.

"For a while," Roseanna said softly, "but I apologized to Him and everything is okay now."

"I'm glad, mommy," she said, stifling a yawn.

"How did you survive all those months on that island?" Roseanna asked, looking at Brad.

"Big Jake took care of us," Isabelle piped up. "His face is hurt and we're going to help him get it fixed."

"Who's Big Jake?" Roseanna asked, looking again at Brad.

"I'll tell you all about it later," he said.

"Mommy, I love you," Isabelle said for the umpteenth time.

Roseanna pulled her daughter into her arms. "Oh, my precious angel, I love you too. I never thought I would get to hold you in my arms again, see your beautiful face, or hear the sound of your voice," she cried, hugging and kissing her with all her might. "I missed you so much."

"I'll never leave you again, Mommy, I promise," she said, trying to hold her eyes open.

"Lay here beside me, baby," Roseanna said, patting the bed.

Isabelle laid down and snuggled close to her mother. In the matter of minutes she was fast asleep.

Roseanna turned to Brad and took his hand. She leaned up and kissed him. "My darling Brad..."

He pulled away, gently. He touched the wedding band on her hand. "We need to talk about Andy."

"You know about Andy," she gasped.

He nodded his head. "I wanted you to be the first to know that we were alive, so I called your parent's house to find out where you were, and Lee told me that you had gone to the church to marry Andy, and then to the hospital to get the baby."

A tear trickled down Roseanna's face. "Oh, Brad, I'm so sorry you had to hear about it that way. If only I could have told you..."

"It really doesn't matter who broke the news to me, the thing that matters is that it's true." He shook his head. "Sweetheart, I don't understand," he said, his voice trembling.

She took his hand and looked pleadingly into his eyes. "Listen, to me, Brad. Please let me explain..."

"Honey, I peeked in on Will and he's sleeping," Andy said, stepping into the room. "Oh, I didn't know you had company. I'm Andy Winslow, Roseanna's..." He stumbled backwards and the color drained from his face as he looked at the man sitting there. "You're Brad," he gasped, not able to believe what he was seeing.

"Andy, it's a miracle," she exclaimed, "a wonderful miracle. They're alive. God bought them back to us."

Brad looked at the man standing there, the man whose wedding band was now on Roseanna's finger; and hatred came over him, hatred for this man who had stolen his one true love. He knew it was wrong to hate, but he had no control over his feelings. He suppressed an urge to knock Andy across the room. "I think you'd better leave," he said harshly. "This is a private conversation between my—between Roseanna and me, and there is no place here for you."

Andy turned to leave. Roseanna reached out and grabbed his hand. "Please, don't go," she said.

"Then I will leave," Brad said angrily, and stormed out the door.

"Brad, don't leave, please don't leave me again," Roseanna cried, as he slammed the door behind him. She jumped to her feet. "I've got to go after him. I've got to explain."

Andy grabbed her. "You get back in bed," he said. "I'll go after him. I'll make him come back." He hurried out the door and caught up to Brad just as he was getting into his car. He grabbed his arm. "You're not leaving her like this," he said firmly.

"Get out of my way," Brad threatened angrily.

"Go back in there and listen to her, please," Andy said. "Don't do this to her. She loves you…"

"She loves me. Then why is she wearing your wedding band instead of mine? Now, for the last time, get out of my way," Brad said. "Tell Roseanna I'll get in touch with her," he added, revving the engine.

"You're a fool if you walk away from her," Andy shouted over the noise. He shook his head sadly as Brad spun out of the parking lot. He walked back into the hospital room.

Roseanna could tell from the expression on his face that Brad was gone. "What have I done to him?" she cried. "Brad is the kindest, most gentle person, I know. He would never lash out at anyone the way he did at you. He's hurting, and I've got to go to him. Where did he go?"

Andy shook his head. "He didn't say, he just said he'd be in touch with you."

Roseanna got out of bed and headed for the closet.

"What are you going to do?" Andy asked.

"I'm pretty sure I know where he's headed, and I'm going to him. I've got to explain things. I've got to make him understand."

"You're in no shape to be up," he pointed out. "You've just had a baby. You need to stay in bed."

"I'm going to Brad," she said, taking the wedding gown from the closet. Roseanna had gone into labor at the church and they rushed her to the hospital, still wearing her wedding gown. "I've got to get to Brad right away. I won't lose him again."

"Honey, tell me where he is and I will send Belle and Jesse to talk to him…"

"No," she said, "I've got to go to him. He won't listen to anyone else. Just tell the nurse that I'm leaving." She shooed him out the door. She slipped into the wedding dress. She felt strange and out of place wearing it now. How would she explain all this to Brad? Could she make him understand?

"Roseanna, you can't leave until we get the doctor's okay," the nurse said, following Andy back into the room.

"Then I guess, officially, I will still be here," Roseanna said, as she headed out the door. "Andy, call Belle and Jesse and tell them what's going on."

"You're not going out there alone, this time of night," Andy told her. "I'll drive you."

"I'll be perfectly safe," she assured him. "I need you to be here for the baby, and watch Isabelle until Belle gets here. Don't worry, I'll be fine."

Roseanna's thoughts were troubled as she drove down the highway that led to the bayou. "Lord, please let him be there," she prayed. If only he had let her explain. Tears ran down her face. Had she found him, only to lose him again; this time forever. The cell phone rang, cutting into her thoughts. Her heart skipped a beat. The baby.

Had something happened to little Will? She answered it anxiously.

"Roseanna, this is Jesse. Andy called and told us the wonderful news about Brad and Isabelle. He also told us about the problem with Brad. I thought you might need some help..."

"Thanks, Jesse, but, I've got to talk to Brad alone. "I've got to make him understand," she said. "I saw a side of him tonight that I never saw before and it scared me."

"He's been through a lot," Jesse said. "He's hurting, so tread carefully when you talk to him. Let him know how much we all love him."

"I will," she said. "I'm coming to the church now. There's a car parked out front. It's probably his rental car. Talk to you later." She hung up the phone and pulled the car into the churchyard. She jumped out of the car and hurried to her special place. Brad was sitting on the log where they had sat the first day she met him. She went over and sat down beside him.

"Brad, I'm so sorry," she said, tears streaming down her face.

He stood to his feet. "What are you doing here? Shouldn't you be in the hospital?"

"I had to come and find you," she said, standing to her feet, tottering back and forth as a wave of weakness hit her.

Brad grabbed her. "You need to be in bed," he said. "I'm taking you back to the hospital."

"No, take me home," she told him.

"Where is home now?"

"Our home, Brad, the parsonage. I still live there."

"Where does the new pastor live," he asked a bit puzzled.

"We don't have a new pastor yet, the people couldn't bear having someone else in your place so Brother Trosclair

210

has been taking care of the church," she explained. "They did ask Andy to be the pastor..." She stopped short, wishing she had not mentioned that.

Brad scowled angrily. "Not only did he steal my wife, but he stole my church as well."

"Brad, it's not like that at all. Andy would never do such a thing," she declared. "They asked him to be pastor, thinking you were dead. Now, that you're back..." She suddenly felt flushed. Her knees buckled under her and she fell limp in his arms.

"I'm taking you home right now," he said, picking her up and carrying her the short distance to the parsonage. He carried her to their bedroom and laid her down on the bed. He got a wet cloth and placed it on her forehead.

She smiled at him with a weak smile. "This reminds me of the day we met, and I fainted in your arms in front of the whole congregation. You took good care of me that day, too."

He smiled, remembering. "That was some day," he said, "it changed my life forever. Now, you lay back and rest. I'll be in the living room if you need me."

A pain went through her heart. He was acting like a polite stranger. He had not even kissed her once, except the kiss to wake her. It suddenly dawned on her; she had called him Andy! How that must have hurt him. "Oh, Brad, we've got to talk," she said, taking his hand. "I'm sorry, baby, I'm so sorry. Please forgive me."

"We'll talk tomorrow."

"No, we'll talk now," she said. "Come sit here beside me. There's some things you've got to know, and they won't wait 'til tomorrow."

He sat down on the bed. "Roseanna, I don't think you're up to this."

"I'll be fine," she said. "But I do want to get out of this dress."

"You look beautiful," he said. "I'm sure you made a stunning bride."

"About that, Brad..."

"Which gown do you want," he asked, ignoring her comment and walking to the dresser.

"It doesn't matter," she said, a tear rolling down her face. He was so distant. Could she make him understand?

He picked out a soft blue gown and got her robe out of the closet. He handed them to her.

"Would you please unfasten these buttons on the back of my dress? I can't reach them."

As he unfastened the buttons, he wanted to take her in his arms and kiss her. His mind went back to another time, long ago in the churchyard, when he had kissed her on impulse, before remembering that she had married the prince the day before. He'd felt as if he had committed the mortal sin, that day, by kissing a married woman. She wasn't married, then, as it turned out; but today she *had* married Andy, and bore his son. He wasn't sure about the legality of the marriage, but Roseanna had promised herself to another man, and he would respect those vows she made. He unfastened the last button and turned his head while she changed into the gown.

She pulled the robe on over the gown. Another tear slid down her cheek, as she saw him turn away. Did he hate her so much that he couldn't stand the sight of her? She had to try to get through to him. "Brad, we need to talk about Andy..."

"Where is he? What kind of man would allow you to drive here, alone at night, in your condition," he said, his jaw twitching angrily.

"He's at the hospital with the baby..."

"I should have known," Brad said, a bit sarcastically. He sat down on the bed beside her. "Roseanna, do you love Andy?"

212

She couldn't lie to him. "Yeah," she said, a catch in her voice, "I love him, but..."

"Then I will walk out of your life, forever."

"No, Brad," she replied, shocked that he would suggest such a thing.

"I don't want you staying with me out of loyalty, or guilt, or because you think it's the right thing to do. I don't want you that way," he told her firmly.

She fought back the tears. What was happening here? Had he stop loving her? If not, where was that man who would fight for the woman he loved 'til the day he died. This man was like a total stranger to her. Where was the Brad she loved?

"Brad, help me to understand," she cried. "Don't you care anymore? Where is all your compassion? You haven't even asked about the baby."

"I'm sorry," he said, "I truly hope the baby is okay. I know sometimes premature babies don't fare too well. Forgive me, Roseanna, I should have asked."

"Premature?" she asked. "Premature," she stated again in disbelief. "What's going on in that mind of yours, Bradley Lefourche?" She was beginning to get his drift and she was getting angry.

"Roseanna, I've been gone eight months, and for you to have, even a premature baby this soon, you had to turn to another man within two weeks of the accident. How could you do that?"

"Is that what you think?" Her words were cold. "How could you think I would do such a thing?" She started weeping hysterically, thinking back to that horrible night when Daddy and Jesse had come home without Brad and Isabelle. "How could you think such a thing, Brad?" she cried again, heartbrokenly. Sobs gushed from her throat and shook her whole body.

Brad pulled her into his arms. "Don't cry, sweetheart, please don't cry."

"It's no use," she sobbed, pulling away from him. "If you think I could do that..." Her voice quivered as her heart broke inside her. "It's over between us, Brad. If you believe I could do such a thing, then, there's nothing left to hold on to. Please, just go and leave me alone."

"No, I won't go," he said determinedly. "I'm staying right here." He took her in his arms again.

She was too tired to argue. She closed her eyes and fell asleep, cradled in his arms.

Brad reached over and switched off the light. He lay there, staring into the darkness, trying to sort things out in his mind. Why was she so angry with him? He was the injured party here. He should be the angry one, and he was. He was angry most of all with Andy for taking advantage of Roseanna. He was angry with her for turning to another man so quickly. He was even angry with God for keeping his hopes alive all those months on the island. As he lay there, holding her in his arms, tears streamed down his face. He pulled her close and kissed her tenderly. He loved her so much. How could she stop loving him so soon? Their love was going to last through all eternity, but for her, it didn't even last one year. She loved Andy. He had to accept that. Andy was the father of her baby, her son. That really hurt. He and Roseanna had wanted a son for so long; now she had one, by another man. More tears slid down his face. She was right; it was over between them. He could have fought against the love she felt for Andy; but he couldn't fight against that baby boy who needed both his mother and father. "Goodbye, Roseanna," he whispered, kissing her again, and easing off the bed. He walked into the living room and sat down in his recliner. He didn't want to leave her alone so he would stay here tonight. Tomorrow, they would say their final goodbyes, and he would walk out of her life forever. He would give her the chance to find happiness with Andy, and the son that bonded them together.

When Roseanna awoke the next morning her first thoughts were of Brad and Isabelle. They were alive! She remembered going to sleep in Brad's arms. She reached over to touch him. The bed was empty. "No," she whispered as the truth hit her. It *was* just a nightmare. They *were* dead. "No!" she screamed, her heart bursting with pain. "Brad! Isabelle!"

Brad awoke, when he heard her scream. He ran into the bedroom and gathered her in his arms. "Sweetheart, what's wrong," he asked, his heart pounding furiously.

"Brad," she gasped, "when I woke up and you weren't here, I thought last night had just been a terrible nightmare, and you and Isabelle were really dead. Oh, Brad, hold me. Please hold me. Don't ever let go of me." She trembled in his arms.

"I'm here, sweetheart," he said, holding on to her tenderly.

"Oh, Brad, I love you so much," she cried, leaning up and kissing him with a passion that she hadn't felt since he left that day, eight months ago.

He kissed her back, and in that moment everything else left his mind. His precious Roseanna was back in his arms. How good it felt to be holding her again. Then he remembered. Andy---the baby.

"Roseanna, the baby," he said, as reality set in. "The baby needs his father..."

"I know," she answered, kissing him again, "and I'm going to make sure he gets his father."

"Then, we can't be here in each others arms," he said, stepping away from her.

"Brad, you haven't even asked what the baby's name is," she said.

"Andy called him Will…"

"His full name is William Bradley Lefourche," she continued, "and he's not premature."

Brad stood there, stunned. The truth dawned on him. "Then, that means---I'm his---he's my…"

"Yes, Will is your son, our son, the little boy we always wanted," she said, through tears of joy. "I didn't know it, but I was almost a month pregnant when you went on the fishing trip."

He scooped her up in his arms and let out a whoop of joy. He kissed her over and over. Then he gasped in horror. "Oh, Roseanna, the things I accused you of. I'm so sorry. Can you ever forgive me?" He fell to his knees and wept. "Sweetheart, I don't deserve you, but I'm begging you to give me another chance. Please, don't cut me out of your heart."

"I couldn't cut you out of my heart even if I wanted too, my darling, and I do understand your feelings," she said lovingly. "You were stranded on that island for months and when you finally get home, you find me wearing another man's wedding band, and having a baby. What else could you think?"

"I could have trusted you," he said.

"We're together now, that's the most important thing;" she said, "but we do need to talk about Andy. There are some things I need to explain." She held out her hand, showing Brad there was no wedding band. "I took it off last night."

"Sweetheart, you married Andy thinking I was dead," he said. "You took those vows in good faith, you had every right to do so---and you do love him…"

She cupped her hand over his mouth. "I've been trying to explain, honey, I'm not married to Andy. We never took our vows. We did the giving of the rings first. As soon as he placed the ring on my finger, I went into labor, and we rushed to the hospital. Andy wouldn't take time to finish the ceremony 'cause he didn't want to put me, or the baby, in jeopardy. I'm still your wife. I'm still Mrs. Bradley Lefourche."

They stood there, in each other's embrace, and the eight months that they were separated faded dimly into the past. The tears of mourning had turned into tears of joy as they pledged their love once again. Roseanna took the locket out of her purse and handed it to Brad.

His heart overflowed with rapture as he unfastened the locket and took the wedding band off the chain. He clasped the locket around her neck and slipped the ring on her finger. "With this ring I thee wed," he said, kissing her with all the love and passion inside him.

"I love you, and only you," she vowed, "now and forever."

"Throughout all eternity," he added.

"About me loving Andy," she said, feeling the need to explain it to Brad. "My love for him is real, but I fell in love with him thinking you were dead and lost to me forever. When you walked into that hospital room, everything between Andy and me was over. You are my one true love, Brad, and you, alone, will possess my heart forever. The hardest thing I ever had to do was to say goodbye to you and Isabelle; but I finally realized I had to let you go. So one night a couple of months ago, I went to the ocean and put flowers in the water as a memorial to you and our daughter…"

"Pink and yellow roses?"

"How did you know?" she asked.

"They floated to the island and Isabelle found them in the water. Isabelle's favorite color is pink and there were yellow roses at our wedding, so I thought that the flowers was a message from you, that somehow God had sent them to let us know that you were thinking of us. I had no idea that you had put them there."

The tears streamed down Roseanna's face as she thought of how God had worked in their lives. "Oh, Brad, God is so good. He tried to keep the spark of hope burning in my heart, that you were still alive, and I held on for a long time; but, eventually, I let my head override my heart; if only I'd known how to trust Him more."

"That's my fault, sweetheart," he said, "I made it too easy for you to lean on me instead of leaning on God."

"That's one good thing that has come out of all of this. "I've learned how to trust in God for myself. I've become stronger in my faith."

"And, another good thing that came out of this is Big Jake," Brad added. "Without Isabelle and me being there on the island with him, he might never have found the Lord, again, and received the strength he needed to come home."

"And those two people at the concert whose lives were changed by the new song..." She paused. "Brad, do you think God caused all of this to happen?"

"I don't think so," he answered thoughtfully. "I believe it was just a horrible accident. God took a bad situation, and caused good to come from it."

"Look at the time," she muttered, glancing at the clock. "I've got lots more to tell you, but right now, we've got to get back to the hospital. Our kids need us."

"Just think," Brad said, his heart swelling with pride, "in a few minutes I will be holding my son in my arms. Do you know how happy that makes me, Roseanna?"

She nodded and squeezed his hand.

"I misjudged Andy," Brad said on their way back to the hospital. "I need to apologize."

"Andy understands," she told him. "He knows how much we love each other. The moment he saw you standing there, he knew, in that one glance, that he had lost a wife, a son, and a church; but he wouldn't change a thing. That's the kind of man he is. I love you, my darling husband, with all my heart, but I can't forsake Andy. He was there when I needed him. I've got to be there for him now."

He pulled her close. "I understand, sweetheart. I know that Andy is no longer a threat to our love. I know he must be hurting, and we will do everything we can to help him get through this."

Her eyes lit up. Her heart was filled to overflowing. Brad was back to his old self. Her heart was singing as she sat beside him with her head on his shoulder. Her life was so wonderful, so perfect. God had brought Brad and Isabelle back to her, and had given them that precious baby boy. They would be going home later today as a family. The house that had held so much sadness and grief for the past eight months would ring again with their voices and happy laughter. "Thank You, God," she whispered, snuggling closer to Brad. God had walked with them through this dark valley and brought them here, beyond the tempest, into the sunshine of their love for each other, and into the brightness of His eternal care. "Thank You, God," she whispered again, basking in the comfort of His presence, and in the warmth of Brad's love.

Books in Roseanna Series

Roseanna
Belle's Restless Heart
Beyond The Tempest
Rainbow's End (coming soon)

For more information on books
and
To hear samples of music from John Houston, writer of the song, *Roseanna,* from which the book, *Roseanna,* was written. This music includes songs sung by Roseanna in the books.

Visit our website:
www.royalfamilymusic.com

Worship background tapes and CD's also available.

Songwriters, visit this site and see the opportunities offered to you.

E-mail: gohouston@hotmail.com
E-mail: goviti@hotmail.com